**Celebrate Lass Small's 50th title
for Silhouette Books with another
unforgettable story in her series:**

*Every book's a keeper in this sexy saga of
untamable Texas men and the stubborn beauties
who lasso their hearts.*

You met sweet-talkin' Rip and his lovely lady Lu in

TAKEN BY A TEXAN
(Desire #1137)

And who could forget the wonderful romance
between Andrew and JoAnn in

THE HARD-TO-TAME TEXAN
(Desire #1148)

Now that infamous bachelor Tom Keeper finally
gets his own chance at romance in

THE LONE TEXAN
But will bright-eyed beauty Ellen be the girl to
change his mind about love and marriage? Read on
to find out…and read a personal message from
author Lass Small herself!

Dear Reader,

This month, Silhouette Desire is celebrating milestones, miniseries—and, of course, sensual, emotional and compelling love stories. Every book is a treasured keeper in Lass Small's miniseries THE KEEPERS OF TEXAS, but this month, the continuation of this wonderful series about the Keeper family marks a milestone for Lass—the publication of her 50th book for Silhouette with *The Lone Texan,* also our MAN OF THE MONTH selection!

Desire is also proud to present the launch of two brand-new miniseries. First, let us introduce you to THE RULEBREAKERS, Leanne Banks's fabulous new series about three strong and sexy heroes. Book one is *Millionaire Dad*—and it's a story you won't want to miss. Next, meet the first of a few good men and women in uniform in the passion-filled new series BACHELOR BATTALION, by Maureen Child. The first installment, *The Littlest Marine,* will utterly delight you.

Continuing this month is the next book in Peggy Moreland's series TEXAS BRIDES about the captivating McCloud sisters, *A Sparkle in the Cowboy's Eyes.* And rounding out the month are two wonderful novels—*Miranda's Outlaw* by Katherine Garbera, and *The Texas Ranger and the Tempting Twin* by Pamela Ingrahm.

I hope you enjoy all six of Silhouette Desire's love stories this month—and every month.

Regards,

Melissa Senate

Melissa Senate
Senior Editor Silhouette Books

Please address questions and book requests to:
Silhouette Reader Service
U.S.: 3010 Walden Ave., P.O. Box 1325, Buffalo, NY 14269
Canadian: P.O. Box 609, Fort Erie, Ont. L2A 5X3

LASS SMALL
THE LONE TEXAN

SILHOUETTE *Desire*®
Published by Silhouette Books
America's Publisher of Contemporary Romance

If you purchased this book without a cover you should be aware that this book is stolen property. It was reported as "unsold and destroyed" to the publisher, and neither the author nor the publisher has received any payment for this "stripped book."

 SILHOUETTE BOOKS

ISBN 0-373-76165-1

THE LONE TEXAN

Copyright © 1998 by Lass Small

All rights reserved. Except for use in any review, the reproduction or utilization of this work in whole or in part in any form by any electronic, mechanical or other means, now known or hereafter invented, including xerography, photocopying and recording, or in any information storage or retrieval system, is forbidden without the written permission of the editorial office, Silhouette Books, 300 East 42nd Street, New York, NY 10017 U.S.A.

All characters in this book have no existence outside the imagination of the author and have no relation whatsoever to anyone bearing the same name or names. They are not even distantly inspired by any individual known or unknown to the author, and all incidents are pure invention.

This edition published by arrangement with Harlequin Books S.A.

® and TM are trademarks of Harlequin Books S.A., used under license. Trademarks indicated with ® are registered in the United States Patent and Trademark Office, the Canadian Trade Marks Office and in other countries.

Printed in U.S.A.

LASS SMALL

finds living on this planet at this time a fascinating experience. People are amazing. She thinks that to be a teller of tales of people, places and things is absolutely marvelous.

Dear Reader,

This is a milestone for me in that Silhouette is celebrating my 50th book published by them. It is a marvel.

I was always told that I should write. My mother and my teachers all commented on that. Instead, I got married and had kids. It wasn't until our third was twelve that I went back to art school.

In the early '80s *everybody* was scrambling for publication, because suddenly all of the publishing houses were launching romances. Home with a little boy, idle, I was already writing short stories and novels. And being turned down.

Finally, I published several books with another house. Then I was asked to write a book for Silhouette. I was surprised. I said, "You've turned down five of my books." And that editor replied, "We've matured."

Now, how could anyone ignore that kind of response? I laughed, and she had me.

All of the publishers have been very kind to me, and I salute them all. Of course, Silhouette Books is now my publishing home. I don't know how they manage to find such kind editors. My current editor is Melissa Jeglinski. She is another jewel.

Obviously, my mother and my teachers were right all along. I was fortunate to be where I was, at the time the opportunity was open, and I've been especially fortunate in editors. It has been a pleasure.

With writer's love,

Lass

One

On the Keeper ranch in northwest TEXAS, the problem with the senior Mrs. Keeper was that she could never really, actually abandon anybody. She simply could not quit, give up or let any of them go, for crying out loud.

That was why she spent so much time…enduring people. She was so earnest that the most recalcitrant person finally just gave up and relaxed and allowed her to—well, actually, she reprogrammed their brains.

It wasn't easy.

However, no person who landed at the Keeper place in northwest TEXAS ever left there for good.

That immediately gives an observer the sound of a closing tomb like in an Egyptian pyramid. And one considers the dead pharaoh and the trapped, live wives and servants who were sealed inside the tomb with the corpse.

Well, with Mina Keeper, it wasn't that way. Not at all. It was just that Mrs. John Keeper, Sr., couldn't allow a misdirected human to be rejected. In her mind, *every*one could be straightened out and made logical. Sure.

Mina Keeper was picky. Everybody has their own little quirks. First, Mina learned in which direction was their own stance. Everybody has one. Most of those she monitored were hostile or self-protective.

Off the big dining room was a small, private dining room. It was there that Mina had lunch with the individual ones, subtly directing their table manners. To her, table manners were prime.

Oddly enough, one of her current isolated lunch partners was her own son, Tom. He'd been turned down by women so many times, by then, that he'd decided to be a loner. He was silent and somewhat bitter.

Tom was the version of always a groomsman, never the groom. He'd just stood up with yet another pair who were married. The married couple included Andrew Parsons, a man who had been lost in time; and JoAnn Murray who had—almost—abandoned the time laggard.

Andrew, the time laggard, had a sister, Lu, who was living in one of the houses on the ranch with one of the ranch pilots, Rip. Mrs. Keeper was sure no young woman should live in sin. The fact that Lu was living on the Keeper land, with Rip, was another weight on Mina Keeper's shoulders.

In their bedroom, John Keeper told his wife, Mina, "It's their business."

And Mina said rather woefully, "They're so young."

"They're old enough to decide their own lives. They are deciding if they match."

She turned her head and smiled at her husband on his back, sideways across their bed. "We did that."

"Hush. The walls have ears!"

She laughed in her throat in the way a woman does when a man pleases her, and—

Well, that finished that mind-irritating subject—for a while.

It was several busy days later when an old friend from school, Jenny Little Drew, called Mina Keeper. They laughed and gossiped and exchanged memories, then Jenny mentioned, "Remember Maggie Williams Simpson? Her woebegone daughter, Ellen, needs a place to heal."

"Physical?"

"Everything."

"Uh-h-h..."

"Ellen is not dangerous. She's just silent and wants to be alone."

Mina Keeper gasped, "Out *here?*"

"I've always considered the Keeper Place as a haven."

Mina mentioned with some stridence, "I've always thought you were a little strange."

Jenny was very serious and said into the telephone, "Ellen needs a haven in which to heal."

"What happened to her?"

"A man abandoned her some time ago when he found she was...with child. She lost the baby. Two losses. Him and then the baby. It was too much."

"The bastard."

Jenny was silent a blink. "Why...I'd never realized you knew that word."

Mina replied with some lack of endurance, "I know them all. Send her to us. We'll see if we can help."

In a wavering voice, Jenny said softly, "Ahhh. Thank you. I—hoped—you—could—"

Stridently, Mina warned, "Don't you *dare* bawl on me. I can't survive something like that!"

Jenny's laugh then was water logged.

The odd guest, Ellen Simpson, arrived three days later! She was like a mouse in a houseful of cats. Under a wide-brimmed hat, her hair was dark and rolled into a severe knot at the back of her head.

At least Ellen hadn't shaved her head, but she was withdrawn and silent so that she wouldn't be noticed.

Greeting Ellen, Mina sent a rather strong negative thought to her old school chum Jenny who had very recently become an ex-friend. Unfortunately, Jenny was the kind who never noticed she'd been rejected and abandoned.

Mina smiled gently and said to Ellen, "We are so pleased you could come visit. We have just the room for you." Mrs. Keeper grinned and lifted her eyebrows as she added, "The crew was delighted to straighten the room. I do hope it's something you like. If not, we have other choices.''

''It'll be fine. Mother is especially pleased you invited me here.''

Ellen wasn't? Mina smiled. To her the woman-child even looked like a reject. Mina said, ''Let's see if you like the room's view. If you'd prefer another view, we'll find you another room.''

That gave the guest a reason to see the room and to look outside. Mina always did that to reluctant guests. The choice gave them more liberty and control. She'd had reluctant guests who'd moved immediately, and eventually moved back into the original room.

Mina Keeper acted as if she had the whole day to visit and consider rooms. Ellen didn't remove her hat for some time. She was hiding? Mina was glad that she knew the circumstances of Ellen. At least that allowed Mina to understand the withdrawn young woman.

Gradually, gradually, Mina began to understand this woman who'd been rejected by a man she most probably loved. A woman who had also lost her child. Here was a suffering woman who didn't know how to cope with her losses. And Mina wondered how *she* was to help Ellen?

Mina looked at the sundered girl-woman and her emotions wanted to hold the raw, vulnerable girl and cry with her.

Perhaps at a later time.

Mina showed Ellen the house in a lazy, easy manner. They walked slowly so that the very thin Ellen wouldn't be totally exhausted. They had morning tea, but she gave Ellen milk.

A clue was that Ellen drank some of the milk slowly and didn't appear to even know what she did was guided by her upbringing of courtesy. Someone had given her a tea, she'd had milk handed to her and she did not reject it but had courteously sipped it so as not to embarrass the hostess.

Ellen was given a square cookie that was loaded with good foods and laced with raisins and nuts. She actually ate one. It took a while.

How strange it was to Mina that she watched and waited for a guest to actually eat something, when all her years she'd been overwhelmed with hungry people who talked as they ate.

This guest was mostly silent.

Ellen looked at the things Mina mentioned and indicated, but she had no comment.

It was obvious that Ellen's mother had raised her to be courteous. She endured. How long could Mina keep Ellen by her side? When would Ellen ask to go to her room?

Ellen's first indication was when she mentioned, "I need to lie down."

But before that happened, she fainted!

Anyone who lives out as far from civilization as the Keepers, is schooled in basics. And it was a miracle that the Keepers had good M.D.'s not even three city blocks' distance away.

Mina called. The female doctor came immediately. Dr. Jane Wilkins gave the guest a quick check.

The house helpers were muscular males who lifted Ellen. It was they who quite easily carried the girl to her room.

When Ellen woke, she was in a nightgown, in bed. An intravenous bottle was putting fluid into her system.

Dr. Jane smiled and said, "You're okay."

"I'm sorry I…" Ellen's voice dribbled off.

Softly Dr. Jane said, "No problem."

"I—don't know why I did that."

"Your body has apparently been through a tough time, and you're not yet ready to do much. This is the perfect place to be—to recover. When you're up and around, you could come to the clinic. It's not far, a couple of blocks, and we'll see what kind of vitamins you might need—or if you need any at all."

"I'll probably go home."

Dr. Wilkins said, "Not right away." And she smiled. "Mina Keeper said if your momma heard of that, she might be upset."

The mouth on the white face on the bed smiled just a tad.

"You *are* all right as far as I can see now. Are there any reasons you might be fragile?"

"I…lost a baby."

"That takes some getting over. Relax. Sleep. Contact us at the clinic if you need anything at all. Believe me when I tell you, you could not be in a better place, right now. Come to see us in two days, or I can come back then. We'll be in touch."

A big tear leaked out of the side of Ellen's eye.

Dr. Jane blotted Ellen's temple gently. "You're okay. Call anytime. We're here for you, too. Of course, we also take care of the horses and cattle and what the dickens else is around and ailing. Once it was a buzzard. I've never cottoned to buzzards. Fortunately, one of the male doctors was fascinated. Males are odd. But we do the dogs and cats. We're stretched. We won't actually put a human in one of the animal restraints."

Ellen's eyes were filled with unshed tears but she did smile.

Softly, Dr. Wilkins said, "You are okay."

"Thank you."

"Sleep for two hours. That's the limit. Then you'll sleep tonight—like a log—and tomorrow will be easier. We'll keep the bottle here until it's empty. The Keepers can handle intravenous tubes. No problem." Dr. Wilkins smiled. "I'll check you later. Rest."

Ellen almost smiled. Another tear slid out of the side of her eye.

The doctor said, "Hah! The intravenous must be filling you up. You're overflowing!"

She made Ellen smile but Ellen leaked another tear.

"No more tears," the doctor ordered. "Tears upset us."

That made Ellen grin widely, but another tear slid out.

Blotting that casually, the doctor said, "I'll be back to release you from that gadget. Behave. No dancing. No arguing with these stubborn people around here. Be logical and quiet. I'll be back."

Now...how many times had the doctor said she'd be back? What a pushover she was. She washed her hands, snapped her case together and grinned at her patient as she left.

One of the male hands sat with Ellen. Drowsily, she wondered what she'd do if she needed to go to the bathroom. She watched the slow drip of the water down the tube and she slowly slid into sleep.

Ellen woke again some two hours later. A woman was standing above her bed. She had on plastic gloves and was removing the almost empty jar that had held the dripping fluid.

Somewhat wobbly, Ellen asked, "Are you a doctor, too?"

"Naw. But don't get scared. We all get training in helping each other out here. The doctors over at the clinic give us lessons so we can help one another if we're out and about and they can't get to us right away."

"Oh."

The woman laughed softly but with a great deal of humor. She asked, "Having a clown treat you's a shock, huh?"

That did make Ellen smile. "Yes."

"Don't fret a-tall. We know what we're doing. We have directions. We are all very careful—*because* somebody just might have to do the same thing to us, and we want them to be careful! What goes around, comes around. So *you* might need to help me some time, and I wanna be damned sure I've done you just right!" She laughed.

Even that made Ellen smile.

How long had it been since she'd smiled? And in this strange day now, she'd smiled several times. Would she come to the time when she could be— normal again? And just thinking that she might, another big tear of emotion slid from the side of her eye.

"Now, honey, what the hell's the matter? Did I do something *wrong?* I've—"

"No, no. I haven't—laughed—in some time. You see— Well— Things have been—" And she stopped.

"Never you mind. Everybody has troubles. All we gotta do is look on beyond our own selves. It ain't easy, but if you can, you can see who all needs help. Then you know no matter what all happens, if you can breathe and eat and eject, you ain't bad off a-tall."

How strange such words sunk into Ellen's understanding. She had heard variations of such many times, but it was this woman, whom she did not know, who said what Ellen needed to hear and she'd assimilated the words.

It was only then that Ellen considered herself. She was not healed, as yet, but she was on a better track than that in which she'd been trapped.

How strange.

But she lay there wondering why she was still on earth, and her baby was not.

That caused the tears to leak out again.

The woman said, "No matter what all's happened

to you, you're okay. Praise the Lord and accept your role in life.''

That set Ellen back a notch. She was not a believer at all, and she didn't like being told that she should accept *any*thing! Her bitterness returned, and she was again hostile to any assistance.

The woman sighed. ''I've probably upset you. Everybody tells me to be quiet. I just go right on and talk every damned time, and I always mess it up. I am sorry if I've upset you—''

''You've been very kind. Don't fret.''

The woman accepted that with a big smile. ''You'll be okay. Everything has its— My God, I'm talking again and I ought to just shut up.''

''Are you married?''

''Naw, but I'm susceptible, and I got three kids. Nice kids. They're independent and sassy and we argue most of the time.''

''I'd bet they're darling.''

''Mostly—strange. A couple of them, I don't know for sure who's their daddies.''

Plural? Daddies? That woman? She must be a very willing—partner.

Ellen considered the woman. She was so open and easy. But then Ellen considered herself, and her foolish acceptance of a man who really hadn't wanted her—permanently. He'd only wanted to taste her. No. To use her.

There was no difference between herself and this woman who was so kindly helping her. As Kipling wrote, ''For the Colonel's Lady an' Judy O'Grady are sisters under their skins." Women are women. There is no difference.

With a token tap on the door frame, Mrs. Keeper came into the room. She helped the other woman remove the needle in Ellen's arm. Mina Keeper smiled and said to Ellen, "You get ice cream. Which kind do you prefer?"

"I don't believe I care for any right now."

The brawn-armed woman put in, "You get a spoonful. You can handle that."

Ellen discarded doing anything as she said, "I'll see."

The woman whose name Ellen did not know put in cheerfully to Mrs. Keeper, "That sounds like she's considering."

Mina Keeper told that person, "Well, Ciggie, we'll just fool her and make her beg for what's left after *we* eat what all we want."

Mrs. Keeper had called the woman—Ciggie.

Ciggie laughed with real delight. "We get all the ice cream?"

"We can't throw it away."

Ellen gave up. "I'll take—"

But Mina sighed. "We'll just have to..."

Ellen was a tad irritated and strident, "I *said*—"

But Mina finished her sentence, "—eat it all."

Ellen became pushy and somewhat annoyed, "I *said* I'd eat those first two spoonfuls."

"Oh." Mrs. Keeper was astonished. "Would you like a taste?"

"You *are* speaking of ice cream?"

"Why...yes." So innocent. Good grief.

Ciggie laughed.

Mina gave the invalid a skimpy two spoonfuls on a tiny plate, while their bowls were enormous!

However, Ellen never did get to see exactly how much they'd actually had, but the two greedy ones licked their lips and made sounds that were not at all necessary!

Then Mrs. Keeper said offhandedly to Ciggie, "I suppose if we're not going to make her ill watching us be this greedy, we really ought to go out into the hall."

Over Ellen's courteous protest, the two just went on out of the room. And Ellen could hear the sound of the spoons in the bowls and the almost silent chit-chat and laughter of the two women.

Very irritating. Really, very irritating.

It wasn't until later that Ellen heard why Ciggie and not a doctor had disconnected Ellen from the intravenous bottle. It seemed some man on the Place had interfered with a bull for some reason, which had annoyed the bull, and the hand's stomach had been ripped open.

The medical team had done the adjusting of the organs and the sewing of the skin. The medics had found the surgery very interesting. The victim was not that pleased.

In just a short time, Ellen began to see and hear all the different things that happened on the ranch. No day was dull. The senior Mr. Keeper sighed with irritation and mentioned to Ellen, "You'd think people would have a little care for themselves!"

He'd said *that* to a woman who'd been ignoring herself? Her fragile body? Someone who hadn't given one damn for anything?

It fascinated Ellen to hear someone like a Keeper be furious and very vocal about carelessness. John Keeper was really irritated. And as he blew off temper, he was looking at *her!*

Was he chiding Ellen, or was he explaining stupidity, or was he just scared that somebody he liked had been hurt?

Ellen thought of her mother. She remembered looking at her mother and seeing her fury with her stupid daughter. And her daddy was there, and he'd hushed his wife. His hand on his wife had been gentle and he'd tried to calm her.

Then he'd turned his hurting eyes to his daughter—

Ellen couldn't think about that right then. She might *never* think of it again.

With Ellen more fragile than they'd first thought, it was the next day the two—Mina and Ciggie— came and said to Ellen, "You're to get up now and go out onto the porch to sit in a rocker and stare at the beauty of the Place."

"I believe I'll sleep a while." That was kindly said and logical.

Mrs. Keeper told her, "The doctor said you are not to sleep during the day, you are to wait for the night. You must get up and move about."

Ellen breathed several times in revolt as she was old enough to do that, but she said, "Yes."

Mrs. Keeper simply looked at her as she would any guest who was difficult and she said, "Ciggie will assist you in rising. She will guide you out to the porch. She will give you a layout of the house and grounds where you will walk. You'll do that until you get used to the place, then you can ride farther."

That wasn't suggestion, it was direction. It had the very strong sense of her mother and father. However, Ellen was not someone these persons could direct. She was a free soul. She could do as she chose.

"Since you have all that water sloshing around inside you, Ciggie will take you to the bathroom first."

"I can take myself."

Mrs. Keeper smiled in a very courteous manner and said, "This time, let us help you. You need to know where to go and the layout of the house and yard. Ciggie will help you today. Call me if you need me."

She left.

Directions. That's what Mina Keeper was doing to Ellen. She was being structured. Their way. Now. Damn.

Having been raised as she was, Ellen did manage to smile at the abandoned Ciggie as she said, "Well, that's clear enough. I feel very like a prisoner."

Not at all taking that as bitterness, Ciggie giggled. "She loves you. You ought to see how gentle she gets when she's mad. Well, she don't get *mad* but she can be—uh—let's see if I can find the word. Yeah. Annoyed.'' That was enunciated just right.

Ciggie made Ellen smile.

Two

With time moving into the middle of another day, it was Ciggie who led the still fragile Ellen down the hall to the side door of the Keeper house. She was careful of the guest. "Are you okay?"

"Fine."

Just the way Ellen said that made Ciggie stop and eye the guest with some squinted doubt.

As happens in romances, Mina's son, Tom, came along right then. He hesitated and looked carefully at the women. Then he asked Ciggie, "She okay?"

Being a sentimental person, Ciggie replied, "You ought to see to her getting out on the porch for some air. Be sure she's in the shade but be surer she's warm." Ciggie grinned and her eyes danced...then she turned away and damned near fled!

That left a fragile Ellen standing there by the closed door, which led onto the side porch.

Tom hadn't actually noticed that Ciggie had left them. His eyes were on the fragile woman. He said, "Tell her I'm a Keeper."

There was no reply, so Tom looked over and found that Ciggie had vanished. She was no where around at *all!* How clever.

Since the two were alone, Tom looked at the guest...whoever she was...and he realized she was seriously fragile. He asked, "Are you going out into the sun?"

She altered the word rather vacantly, "Shade."

Tom waited, but she didn't move, so he suggested, "Let me hold the door for you."

She nodded but she didn't even look at him.

He opened the door, then the screen door and stepped outside as he held it for her.

She almost didn't move. But finally she did step forward so carefully that Tom put out a hand and clasped her elbow to stabilize her.

She murmured, "Thank you."

She didn't look at him or flirt or anything. But she did hesitate.

He took a firmer grip on her arm and led her over to the sun side, and he seated her under a large umbrella that was tall and wide. It was also seriously anchored in the center hole of the table and was not at all movable. Winds only ruffled the fringe around the edge of the big umbrella.

Ellen sat in the shade and again said, "Thank you," dismissing Tom.

Being independent, Tom sat down in another chair and watched her.

He wasn't sure if she was ill or a morning drunk, but there was no smell of liquor. She was skinny and probably had been ailing. Tom wondered who had dropped her off on the Keeper doorstep. The guest had not found the Keepers by herself.

He asked her, "Are you all right?"

She nodded once.

That was supposed to be communication? He frowned at her. If she was sick, why had Ciggie directed her to come outside into the sun on the porch?

He asked the woman, "Do you *want* to be outside? You don't seem strong enough to be out here alone."

"I'll ring the bell if I need help." She indicated the table bell used for refilling glasses or plates.

Tom asked with narrowed eyes, "What meal are you eating?"

"None."

"Then...why are you out here?"

That was a logical question. Their parents were friends. They were in an extended group who commented on others. They were distantly in touch. She managed to move her eyes over and look at Mina's son. "I've met you in San Antonio. You were interested in some woman there."

"Kayla."

"Yes. She would be worth the attention. But she remarried that lawyer."

"Yes."

Then Ellen looked at Tom, having been rejected

herself, and she asked him, "Were you—disappointed she married another man?"

He shrugged. "It happens…one way or another. To a man or a woman." He looked around for someone who might be monitoring this fragile female and, seeing no one, it was he who stayed to be sure she didn't faint, all alone, out on the porch.

It was difficult to see inside the house because the glass was tinted so the sun didn't stream in too pushily. That way, Tom did not see the two women backed away and watching the couple on the porch. The two did not speak. That was because Mrs. Keeper had told Ciggie to hush. Therefore, Mrs. Keeper could strain her ears and listen.

However, it *was* interesting that Mina Keeper hadn't told Ciggie to run along and mind her own business. But while they didn't speak, they both watched the odd couple on the porch.

The reason Mina hadn't told Ciggie to run along was if Tom left and Ellen needed help, Mrs. Keeper could send Ciggie out—casually—and in that subtle way could give help to their guest.

Ciggie knew that was exactly so, but she understood Mrs. Keeper and didn't mind at all. Anything Mrs. Keeper did was logical and planned.

How amazing that Ciggie understood Mina Keeper. Very few others did. Most thought the senior Mrs. Keeper was nosy and intrusive.

Back on the porch, Ellen became relaxed. She actually looked around. She said to Tom, "There's no need for you to monitor me. I'm fine.''

He looked at her in some shock. *She* thought she was…fine? He looked around and considered that the jump off the flat porch was not dangerous for such a stranger. But if she went up the several flights to the attic, she might do serious damage to herself jumping from one of the windows.

Then he looked up and remembered the bars that were braced sideways across the windows in a casual, perfectly spaced row. She didn't have a chance of doing anything drastic.

He considered her. *Was* she in self-danger?

He finally decided slowly that, like life, even in death she wouldn't give a damn. She didn't care one way or the other.

But she'd remembered he had had a serious case of Kayla.

He asked gently, ''That man you used to be with…Philip? He left you?''

She nodded.

''Oh.''

''—and then I lost the baby.''

Tom hadn't known she'd been pregnant. He frowned and looked at her. He told her kindly, ''There was some reason for it. Babies sometimes can't make it. There will be another time for you.''

She slowly turned her head and just looked at Tom with ancient knowledge that he would never understand.

He asked, ''Have you been ill?''

''I forget to eat.''

"Can you walk?"

She considered. "Some."

"Let's go around the porch to the shady side."

She was slow in deciding. She turned her head carefully. She began to leave the chair, and he reached to help her. She said, "I can do this by myself."

Tom rose to his feet and just anxiously watched, his hands ready to catch her fall. He wondered if moving her had been a good idea. Maybe she needed the feeling of the warm, TEXAS winter sun on that side of the house?

She straightened and looked around slowly. She asked, "Which way?"

He could carry her. She didn't *have* to go around to the other side of—

Ellen looked at him in a dead glance and asked again, "Which way?"

Tom had never counted the steps of either way. He glanced up and quickly, mentally judged the distance one way or the other. He said, "This way." It would be around the back.

Watching, inside the house, Mina asked Ciggie, "What the *dickens* is he *doing?*" She was huffy and appalled.

Ciggie replied, "We'll see."

Mina gave Ciggie a deadly look of shock. Well, she had asked the question, and Ciggie had given a logical reply. Mina breathed carefully to soothe herself and moved instantly to see where the hell Tom was taking that fragile child-woman!

The two women hurried to the various places to see...

Tom had lifted Ellen into his arms and was carrying her around the back of the house! Good gravy! If a woman was so fragile that she had to be *carried* then she probably should be in bed!

Tom was stopped along the wall of the porch and was indicating something to Ellen that was on beyond. It was horses. No. It was the Longhorns moving slowly and eating grass. Tom Keeper mentioned, "Their horns must be a nuisance but don't they look elegant?"

Ellen said a nothing, "Mmm." A response, not any opinion.

He grinned down at her lying on his arms and asked, "Not taken with Longhorn Cattle?"

"I had a steak—"

Indignantly, Tom interrupted, "You *ate* one? Don't even *say* it! How could you?"

"—and someone told us it wasn't actually longhorn meat, because you all didn't let *any*body kill a-one of them."

Tom nodded as he said, "That's a fact."

The fragile, pale woman smiled.

He asked softly, "Want to go inside now? You've been out a while."

She said, "All right."

He not only carried her into the house, he asked, "Which way?"

She pointed to a guest room down a hallway on that floor.

Beyond, Mrs. Keeper and her cohort had scurried

so as not to be seen. It was frustrating to them *not* to see what was happening!

As he carried Ellen, Tom offered, "Since I've already learned to carry you, would you like a review of the house? The layout is simple and—"

"This time, I'll just go to my room."

"Have I bored you?"

"Oh, no. I'm just tired."

Not having let her go, he asked, "Along here?"

"Yes. The third door."

He carried her to the door as he said, "I've got to be out and about, but I'll be back for lunch and we'll eat on the south side. Okay?"

She hesitated, then she said, "Okay." But there was no enthusiasm.

His foot nudged her door open as she turned the knob and he carried her across the room and carefully laid her on the made bed. Well, he wasn't cognizant about blankets—and she was dressed.

"Want to change?" He asked that watching her soberly. He smiled. "I could help?"

She lay quietly and barely shook her head as she watched him. She said a formal, "Thank you."

"I'll be back at noon."

"Don't bother. I'll probably sleep."

He grinned. "Too much good TEXAS air?"

She almost smiled as she said, "Yes."

"I'll check on you." Then he didn't leave. He watched her. He said yet again, "I'll be back."

A tear slid out of her eye.

He leaned over her and frowned. "What's wrong." A lead-in, not a question.

Her breaths became disorganized.

He was alarmed and said, "I can take care of anything that bothers you. Just tell me what's wrong."

"I was thinking of the baby I lost." And big old tears slid from her eyes.

He sat down on the bed and lifted her onto his lap. He told her, "That's tough. It makes you want to rail at God, doesn't it? Go ahead. God won't mind. You'll eventually understand it all. That little kid might not have made it later, either. He might have—"

"—she."

"—she might have gotten run over by a car or something awful like that. And the kid just decided it wouldn't be long enough, and you could have another."

She asked, "How do you know?"

Her wet face was against his neck and her thin arms were around his body. He held her on his lap, sitting there on the bed. He replied, "My guardian angel explained it all to me just now."

"I don't believe it."

"You've never talked to your guardian angel? Who do you quarrel with when you want to do something and the guardian shakes his head and says Nuh-uh."

There was silence. Then she said, "What did you want to do that the guardian said not to?"

"It's too long a story to tell you, now. I'll tell you the whole kaboodle another time. Why not lie here a while and snooze. I'll wake you when I come back to lunch."

"We'll see."

"Is it food or me you don't like?"

"Food."

"Well… We'll let you *watch me* eat and you can go on starving."

And again she said, "We'll see."

"Let me see your face. I can wipe tears away real easy."

He leaned back and exposed her to the light. Her eyelashes were wet and her eyes were closed. She was too thin and very pale. His heart squeezed. "You're a nuisance, do you know that? I've got all this work to do and here you are, lying on the bed and wanting atten—"

"I do not! You've been intrusive and bossy and obnoxious!"

He said, "Well, yes. You're fragile and skinny and no threat at all so I could just go ahead and say what I wanted. Do you realize how *seldom* I get to *say* anything I want to?"

"Go nurse the lepers."

"My *grandmother* said that! Who told it to you?"

"My grandmother."

"Well, it's one of those realities that you can't knock down. It's truth. There are always people who are worse off than us. And I think it's real nasty to pull it out at a time of stress and wallop a perfectly upset person with such a comment."

"Me, too."

"You'd rather wallow in being unhappy."

"Yes."

He considered that with some elaborate thoughtfulness before he said, "I can see that. For a while. But the time comes when you ought to let the bad stuff go and look ahead. How long's it been now?"

"Five months and two days."

"Well, I can see you being upset the rest of that sixth month. Then I'll expect you to straighten up."

"Yes."

"But you'll have to begin eating again. You're skin and bones."

"I wanted to die, too."

"Naw. You can't do something like that. Nobody would understand and they'd all be irritated with you. You are strong and you— Hush! I'm talking— and you have to cope. It's a real nuisance but that's the way things work. You cope."

"Damn."

There on the bed, he held her on his lap and rocked gently. He commented, "If you get a quarter of the good stuff, you can't complain. Lots of people have it worse than that. You're killing yourself by not taking care of *you*. That's dumb. No! Stop that! I'm giving you good advice that *I've* had. Straighten up and behave and quit feeling sorry for yourself. Let your lost baby go. Have another. Don't compare them or think the first one would'a been perfect."

With leaking tears, she had to shake her head and smile. She said, "You are so rough. I wonder if you've ever soothed a woman."

"What the *hell* do you think I'm doing *now?* Here—hush—I've spent all this time straightening you out when I was *supposed* to go out and help a mare birth *twins,* and I've let that poor horse do it all by herself with only a dozen or so men with her, and I've given you all this valuable time to straighten *you* out! You've exhausted me. Move over and let me lie down, too. I'm worn to a *nub!*"

She shook her head and laughed through her tears. "You're impossible."

He said, "Since we're in your bed and nobody's around and I'm free, why don't you smooth me down and make me feel better."

She watched him carefully. She said, "Shame on you."

He pried himself up and sighed very dramatically. "I did try."

"Thank you."

"I'll see you at noon. Behave. I'll be back."

She responded, "Don't threaten me."

He tilted his head back and considered her. Then he said, "Not right away." And he patted the top of her head. And he left.

Ellen stayed in her room where she was isolated. She lay quietly and didn't think or anything. She didn't even sleep. But she did glance at the clock.

She ordered her lunch to be brought to her room. The crew did that easily. Mrs. Keeper viewed the tray and added another flower to it. She smiled at the one who would deliver it and said, "Good."

Probably the most irritating thing about Mrs. Keeper was that she knew people, she did research, she contacted old friends of theirs, and she learned everything she needed to know in order to spoil one of her guests.

The tray delivered to Ellen was unusual. It had all sorts of goodies on it. Little samples. This and that. Who could resist?

Ellen was human. She did look over at the tray. She saw there was no napkin on it, so she also saw what was on the tray.

That was the sly way of Mrs. Keeper.

Ellen tasted this and that and ate more than she had in some long time. An apricot here, a kumquat there, a slice of banana, a square of a cut-up sandwich, which held lettuce and some mayonnaise. Little bits and pieces of things. It was all alluring.

Wickedly so.

How was a woman to fade away in grief when someone brought a tray like that?

After noon, Tom came up to see Ellen. An empty tray was outside her door. Her door was not locked. He opened it softly saying, "You here?" But he did go inside her room. She was asleep. He considered her.

If it had been she who'd emptied the tray, it was their first victory. She needed some attention. He'd see to it that others hounded her with such care that she wouldn't notice they were helping her.

He carried her tray back to the kitchen and bragged on the cooks for being so innovative. And he complained because *he* never got anything like that…as an appetizer! He talked to the kitchen crew and got all the various things he wanted to eat while he teased and complained that he was always ignored.

Knowing full well that Tom Keeper had his life...well, his food exactly as he wanted it, the crew only laughed at him...and with him. Tom was very humorous. He was especially so that day. How interesting.

Probably the most intriguing thing that Ellen found in that house was that the Keeper cat jumped up on the porch railing and stretched out to ring the doorbell. That way the cat got attention right away and got inside without having to wait.

Dressed in a shirt and long trousers, Ellen was reading a book the next day and the doorbell rang. Mrs. Keeper called down, "It's probably the cat, would you let him in?"

Ellen did go to the door and opened it but it was a woman her age. She was casually dressed. Her name was Lu Parsons and she was the sister of the throwback Andrew, but Lu lived in one of the ranch houses with the pilot Rip Morris.

Ellen smiled and said, "Come inside. I thought you were the cat."

Lu blinked.

Ellen laughed softly and said, "I know. I wonder, too. But they've told me to answer the doorbell because it might be the cat. They *say* that it reaches over from the railing and presses the doorbell. I just wonder if this is a joke they pull on guests."

Lu grinned. "I'll have to stay now just to see that."

"I'd appreciate the backup. They are probably just

giving us something to think about in this rather isolated place."

Lu considered the idea and then agreed, "You're more than likely right."

Ellen moved slowly to a chair, indicated the other to Lu, and sat carefully.

"Are you all right? I've heard you were skinny as a rail, and you're really elegant. Thin." She considered thin, then she said, "You could use some padding. Have a caramel."

Very sadly, Ellen told her guest, "I lost a baby."

Lu knew that already. In their area, gossip hardly passed the original lips before *every*one had heard it and knew all the details. But Lu didn't say she'd heard that. She said, "I'm sorry."

A great tear trembled on the bottoms of Ellen's eyelashes.

Lu shook her head and told her companion, "Don't you *dare* cry because I will too, and I get blotchy. What's past is past. Look ahead."

In halting words, Ellen said, "I'm not sure I know how to do that."

"Look around and see all the other people who cope or need help."

Ellen replied, "Right now, if I found someone else was grieving, I'd just cry more."

Lu advised, "Go see Angela Becker. She has five kids and a very busy husband who is out and around and not available. She's at her wit's end. The kids are just one year apart. She's going nuts. Why not go over and give her a fifteen-minute break?"

"Fifteen minutes?"

"It would be stark relief for Angela. She could catch her breath. Do it once in the middle of the morning and again in the middle of the afternoon. And, Ellen, do *not* get wishy-washy and stay longer. The fifteen minutes is *all!* Understand?"

"I'm…not sure…exactly *how* to deal with children. How old are they?"

Lu repeated, "Six months to age five."

"My word!"

"I believe she responds to the phenomenon with that same kind of shock. If you do go, she could sit for fifteen minutes, without having to *do* anything or listen to anybody!"

Hesitantly, Ellen confessed with some caution, "I'm not very sturdy."

"Neither is Angela."

Slowly, Ellen rose from her chair and went to the window to look out at the other houses. "Which one is—Angela's?"

Lu went over and pointed out the house. "Want to come along with me and see the house and kids? Then you could decide."

"I'm not at all strong."

"None of us is."

Ellen asked, "Five children and the eldest is just—five?"

Lu nodded. She watched with great interest. How would the fragile woman respond?

Ellen said softly, "I'm not sure—I can handle—someone's—children."

Lu shrugged. "Kids are kids."

Ellen lifted her watery eyes and said, "Yes. They are all precious."

Lu grinned at the weepy woman as she said, "When they're asleep?"

Ellen shook her head, trying to control herself.

"One of these days you'll have to face the fact that there *are*—other children."

"I know."

In another few minutes, Ellen called to Mrs. Keeper who had to take big steps backward so that her voice reply wasn't too close. She innocently asked, "Yes?"

Ellen called back in explanation, "Lu Parsons is taking me over to meet Angela Becker? We won't be long."

Mrs. Keeper called down, "Hello, Lu. How nice of you to call on us. Just see to it that Ellen takes it easy."

Lu called back, "Sure."

Ellen had no clue—at all—that it had all been carefully plotted by those two women.

The two young women got into Rip Morris's car and drove the couple of blocks over to Angela's house. Anyone else would have commented on having to use the car in that short distance, but the fragile Ellen accepted that the drive would be just that.

Angela Becker answered their knock almost before they managed it. She was rather in disarray and her hair was not tidy. She held one child under one arm.

But she was calm and apparently delighted to have guests. She did not appear harassed.

Angela and Lu talked after Ellen had been introduced. As that was being done, a two-year-old came to them yelling bloody murder.

With some effort, Ellen picked that one up. With her lax muscles, the baby weighed a *ton!* She asked soothingly what could be wrong? And the baby didn't squirm out of her hands or arms but babbled baby talk while he pointed.

Ellen carried the little one in the direction he'd pointed, so Ellen missed seeing the exchanged glances made by Angela and Lu who smiled. Angela lifted her eyebrows in pleased shock and stared at Lu.

Lu shrugged, looked at her watch and said in a whisper, "We'll see. Hers was a little girl."

"Ahhh."

The little one in Angela's arm wriggled free and was set down to the floor. She went to see where her little brother and the lady went. So Angela and Lu sat down in the stiff chairs that had been discarded to the entrance hall because nobody liked the chairs.

When fourteen minutes had passed, the two went to find their guest, Ellen. She was sitting on the floor with the children. She was listening to them. They all took turns talking. Ellen had insisted on that and pointed to who was to speak.

The two-year-old spoke gibberish, which the older kids knew and interpreted the gibberish quite easily. The boy was too young with words to correct them.

Lu said, "We have to go."

It was some pang for the two women to watch Ellen carefully rise from the floor. She smiled at the kids. They touched her knees and thighs and said, "Come back." And the little boy said earnest things no adult understood. His littler sister just watched.

The two women, Lu and Ellen, went out of the house, returning the calls of goodbye that they all said, and they went back to the car.

Since they were out, Lu took Ellen to show her Rip's house where she was...uh...shacked up?

She laughed. And Ellen did smile. But Ellen was remembering how much she'd missed her lover when he'd abandoned her.

After their short view of Rip's place, the two women went to the grocery store there that not only sold food but shared all the gossip. And the fact that the Keepers' fragile guest was there awed them all. Lu took it in amused stride.

Mrs. Keeper had commanded Lu to take Ellen to the grocery store. Everyone would be so curious and they'd all find all sorts of excuses to come out to the house. Mrs. Keeper just did not have the time to give teas for all those people! Having the locals see Ellen at the grocery would soothe their curiosity.

It was just lucky that Lu Parsons' brother and his new wife were on their honeymoon. The Keepers' town thrived on gossip.

Three

Ellen was brought back to the Keeper house by Lu. It was obvious Ellen was just about at the end of her strength. It was Ciggie who was at the door first, and she simply took Ellen along to her room, helped her strip and put her naked into bed. She insisted the fragile one drink most of the water in the fresh glass. Ellen did. She handed the glass back to Ciggie. She was asleep in no time at all.

The fact that Ellen was so vulnerable shocked everybody. They'd really just thought she was skinny and grieving. They thought it was primarily attitude. They hadn't realized how far down she'd gone physically.

Mina called Ellen's doctor. When he was free, he returned the call. They discussed the whole situation.

It was rather late that day when Tom came from

a distant check on what was where. His mother updated Tom. He went to Ellen's room and with only one tap, he silently opened her door. He looked inside. She slept. He went over to her bed and watched her sleep. She was flat out. She was exhausted.

But—

Tom found his body wanted to be in her bed with her. How stupid of it. The woman was strained to the core. How could he be that intrusive? Intrusion was what he had in mind.

There was no excuse, at all, for Tom to do anything. He could cough, or clear his throat, or touch her or speak to her. While she was as zonked as she could be, he knew full well that he must not do any of those things. He had to leave her be. She was overextended. He needed to leave her alone and let her sleep until supper time.

But he stood and watched her possessively. He couldn't remember one of the women who'd come to the Keeper Place who had caught his glance as seriously as Ellen did. She made his dreams vivid and sexual. This morning he awoke to a bed that was about torn apart.

How come one woman could do that to a man? He'd lusted for other women. But not with the gentle hunger he had for this one. She'd probably tell him to run along home to his mama and behave himself.

This *was* his home. He was in charge.

That meant that he had discarded the fact that his mother and father ran the Place and were obeyed by the crew without any question at all. How come he felt he was—in charge?

It was this fragile, soul-shaking woman. She made him feel thataway. He'd wanted other women, but it had never been as serious as this want was.

Maybe it was because he'd never seen one in bed before he'd been in there with them? Was it simply the damned old body hunger? Then if that was so, why was he so quiet and why was he just looking at her sleep-closed face?

Why hadn't he thought about her body being in those silks she probably wore like just about every other woman he'd known? He hadn't even thought of it. He'd just known she was asleep. And not being awake, he could look his fill of her face.

Then his vulgar libido wanted to lift the blankets back and look at her body. What was she wearing under those covers thataway? He wanted her nude and raw. He wanted to take off his boots and clothes and even his hat and just get in bed with her and— soothe her. Mmm-hmmmm. That's what he wanted.

When Tom exited Ellen's room, by some miracle there was no one in the hallway. It was silent and empty.

It was almost time for the evening dinner gong. Tom went thoughtfully to his room and stripped easily. His sex, which he referred to as Hunter, leaped free of Tom's underwear, and Tom had several unkind things to say to something so strained.

Ellen didn't rouse from her dead sleep until Mina Keeper went in and told her kindly it was time for her to waken.

Ellen's eyes slitted open. She blinked slowly and

moved her eyes around to figure out where in the world she was. She asked, "Mrs. Keeper?"

Mina gently said, "You're here with us."

Slowly, Ellen commented, "I haven't slept like that in a hundred years."

Mina's eyebrows lifted a tad, and she then had the audacity to comment, "I hadn't known you were older than I."

Ellen blinked slowly and her smile began. "I really slept."

"Yes." How wise the older woman was to only comment and not flood the healing woman with chatter. Mina was simply there.

Ellen lifted the bedcovers from her and was surprised. "I went to bed naked? I've never done that. I must have been very tired."

"You were."

"This bed is like a cloud. A stable one. It didn't dip and wobble."

Mina smiled.

The young woman lay silent. She looked around casually. She said again, "I really slept."

"Ummmm. Your robe is right here. Do you need any help?"

Ellen smiled. "I think I can do it okay."

"Then I'll go on along. The supper gong will be soon. Don't go back to sleep."

"I won't."

Mina Keeper leaned over and kissed Ellen's forehead. She did that for compassion, but she also did it to be sure the child-woman had no fever. She told

Ellen, "I'm glad you could rest. We'll see you at the table." And the lady went on off.

Ellen watched after Mrs. Keeper as she left and closed the door to Ellen's room. Ellen lay quiet and thoughtful. She understood she was healing. She wasn't sure she wanted to heal.

She considered her life and gradually she became aware that the first gong for dinner had vibrated along the hall. She threw back the covers and did a very casual job of rolling up and getting out of the bed.

It didn't even occur to her that she'd done that.

She hadn't time for a shower, so she had a "spit bath," which meant just swishing the washcloth over herself. She donned clothing that was probably okay and brushed her hair back. She viewed herself in the mirror and thought how wimpy she looked. She made a distasteful face at herself and the mirror repeated it. She smiled with humor...and the mirror gently smiled back.

She watched her reflection. She was skinny. How strange that she'd lived all this while and never noticed that she had lost so much weight.

That made Ellen thoughtful as she slowly went out of her door and down the hallway to the dining room. She wondered if she could live after all. Not just be—alive, but to live fully. Until then it hadn't occurred to her that it might be possible. She would see.

One step at a time.

As they were served, Ellen considered the plate.

She recalled the wonderful "tasting" plate Mrs. Keeper had begun to give her not long before. It had been samples of individual bits with all kinds of fruits.

This plate was similar in that it was mostly kinds of main meal gatherings. There was a bit of sweet potato, a bit of ham, of roast beef, of green beans, of salad.

Her partner to the left of her said, "How come you got all them there nibbles, and I just got all this?"

She laughed softly but then she said prissily, "I'm special."

He looked at her.

She grinned at him as she waited for his rebuttal. He was a man in his sixties or seventies.

He replied, "I believe that."

She laughed out loud. She wasn't even aware of it.

But Mrs. Keeper heard and she took a quick, surprised breath. Then her eyes filmed. That annoyed her. So she turned to the person on her right and asked, "Will the rain come?"

That always set off an area male into a long discourse. But she listened. She never just triggered someone's vocal chords, she listened to what they had to say...and she remembered. She also corrected, demurred and agreed.

Tom came in to dinner late. He was there quickly and took off his hat and gave it to somebody who was available. It happened to be a serving man who carried a large tray, but that person simply put the hat on his own head and went right on to what he'd been doing.

Tom got a chair and put it between his father and Ellen. They both moved in order to give him room. His daddy's greeting was, "How come you're late?"

Looking mostly at Ellen, Tom explained about the dammm-arned bull that wanted *all* the cows and was fighting the other bulls.

While that explanation was being made, a plate, silverware and glasses were put before Tom, and he was given a made-up plate that just about overwhelmed the base plate.

Tom allowed himself to be served, and he talked around the food to catch up on everything. He saw that Ellen was more alert! It almost stopped his breathing. It just about took away his hunger for food.

Something clever was said and—she laughed.

That darned near sundered him.

He watched her and his eyes were a little moist. He said, "You're getting sassy. What happened to the gentle, silent woman I met?"

Ellen tilted her head and replied, "She's healing."

Now just those words were very poignant to Tom. He said softly, "Thank God."

"So you like feisty, argumentative women?"

He said, "It's just like everything else. Nothing wants to do what a man wants it to do. Take a horse, for instance. You have to go through mud, and your horse is a nut who doesn't like its hooves to get all dirty."

She laughed.

The others listened and laughed and commented, but he only heard that Ellen laughed. He forgot they weren't alone.

His daddy asked, "I see your plate is clean. I suppose you want some more?"

Tom turned his head in surprise to find his father sitting beside him. He said, "Where'd you come from?"

The whole table laughed.

Tom said, "How come you all don't run along and mind your own business?" He appeared quite logical.

However—

Ellen pushed her chair back and said, "I've finished anyway. If you'd like to be alo—"

Tom told her, "Hush and sit still."

Then somebody down the way asked, "How come we all have to sit still and listen to you?"

Tom considered the man with eyes that were full of hilarity. He told the guest, "I just want to get my own words into this discussion without being entirely left out!"

That made them all laugh.

Ellen asked, "What did you want us to know?"

"You know that dam—arned bull that gets stuck all the time? He got stuck again."

She waited for the laughter to ease off and she asked, "You haven't killed him, have you?"

"One of *our* bulls? Honey—" and his eyelashes became noticeable as he watched Ellen "—that there bull is worth his weight in gold. But he's got to stop getting his valuable parts stuck in mud…yet again. Do you suppose…hush you guys…do you suppose he's overused and needs—"

"Careful." Two male voices cautioned.

His mother said, "Go on."

Tom continued, "—to cool off?"

The men then with eyes that twinkled and danced had to mention things around and about so that they avoided being actually vulgar. It was well-done.

The women laughed but they hushed the men. It was then how clever they could be in *almost* saying things. It was hilarious.

Not only did they laugh, but the crew hovered around and listened and laughed along with them.

John Keeper watched his son with crinkled eyes laughing, but there were tears. Tears could be accepted with such hard laughter, but Mina looked at her husband, and he turned his eyes to hers. They shared the miracle of multirejected Tom coming around and being himself again. He was sassy and…healing.

Then Tom allowed the others to shine as they teased and laughed. It was a wonderful evening. Most of the evening dinners at the Keepers were fun, or soberly interesting, but this one went on beyond that in the parents' hearts. Tom was back with them as he used to be.

Of course, they then looked at Ellen. What if she spurned Tom? What if she wasn't interested in this place and how it was run? What if she simply left there, healing as she finally was?

Then the parents looked at Tom and listened. He

was funny and droll and he listened to the others as they talked and teased. He wasn't only being open to Ellen, he was healing and treating them all as if he knew them and liked them.

It was an emotional time…at least for John and Mina. But they wondered if Tom would be sundered yet again—this time by Ellen.

When the dinner was finally finished, everyone was worn-out from laughing so much. Those limp people were pleasantly exhausted.

Tom said to Ellen, "Get a jacket and let's go out and see if the sky has changed any."

She shook her head as she grinned at him. "I'm exhausted. I haven't laughed that much in an age. I'm going to bed."

With his hands in his pockets, he took a casual step and watched his feet, but he lifted his eyes to her as he asked sassily, "By yourself?"

She looked back over her shoulder and her eyes were wicked. She said, "Absolutely."

Then she wiggled the fingers of one hand in a goodbye manner and went on off.

He watched her out of sight as she turned down the hall to go to her room.

Oddly enough, it was the pilot Rip and his love, Lu, who came up in back of Tom. Rip said, "She's *almost* as interesting as Lu."

Tom smiled at Lu and said, "You'll have to coach her."

Lu blinked. "Coach?"

"So's she'll realize I'm perfect."

Lu considered rather elaborately, frowning for

memory, licking her lips, tilting her head. "Next to Rip, you're not bad."

Rip loved it. Tom was disgusted. He said to the couple standing there, "Prejudice. Prejudice is distasteful."

Rip put out his hands in shock and said, "I'm the best around here, she *said* so! She's told me she's *always* right!"

And smothering the quick laughter, Tom discarded that information quite easily, "Baloney." But his eyes danced and he looked over at Lu.

She tilted her head and lifted her chin. She knew she was right.

Rip took her hand and said so that Tom could hear, "Come on, honey, he's a Neanderthal."

Tom was shocked. "How'd you know that word. It's more than one syllable!"

Preciously, Lu explained, "He's been around... me."

Tom laughed and so did Rip. He took Lu's hand and waved the other to Tom as he tugged her away. She allowed it.

Tom watched them leave. He wondered if Ellen would tease with him? He wondered if she would—see—just him. If the time would come when he could be with her, and she wouldn't mind. She was still fragile, but she was getting stronger. Would she leave?

If he lost her this time, he would probably never see her again. Some other guy would have the time and patience to soothe her and slowly reel her in.

He went to find his dad. He knocked on his parents' bedroom door and his dad answered. He wore only his robe.

Tom grinned and said, "I'll see you tomorrow."

John Keeper said, "Or now?"

"Naw. I just wanted to talk."

John tied his robe and stepped barefooted outside their room's door. "Let's go to that vacant room down the hall. We can talk there instead of the living room, and I'll not look so uncouth."

Tom grinned. "You've never looked *un*couth. You've always been my hero."

His dad looked at his son silently. Then he said with stabled emotion, "I love a child who loves me."

As they walked down the hall to the room, patiently waiting, his dad asked Tom, "How can I help?"

"Talk to me. I need to hear."

"What sort of thing do you need to hear?"

"Just...talk. I can't go upstairs and go to bed. I'm restless. I don't want to walk. I want talk. Just talk. Nothing serious."

"The Cubs will be playing soon."

Tom was shocked, "How can a TEXAN be a Cubs' fan?"

"Damned if I know."

"Then how come *you're* one?"

His daddy shook his head. "I haven't a clue! It...just happened!"

So they talked sports.

How basic. They never mentioned anything else, the ranch, the mystery that still surrounded Andrew

Parsons' shot horse, the people who lived on their land. Nothing else was commented about, just sports.

The time came when Mr. Keeper yawned and almost unhinged his jaw. He was that sleepy. He smiled and blinked like a lazy dog. He said to his son, "It's time for an old man like me to go to bed."

"You've only just reached your apex in this life—"

His father inquired with some interest, "—*this* life? I'll have another?"

That made his son consider, "I wonder if it'll be with Mina."

Tom's daddy said, "I just hope it isn't with some other shrew."

Tom laughed, but the door opened a bit and Mina asked, "Who's a shrew?"

Her husband grinned without his mouth revealing that, but his eyes danced. He told Mina, "A woman I avoided."

Mina said in disgust, "Ginger."

John Keeper sighed, "Her again. Your mother never realizes Ginger was a leech and only your subtle mama could save me."

Tom asked, "How'd she do that?"

"She'd sic the dog on her."

"Our gentle *mother* did that?"

John looked at his wife and smiled. "She's possessive."

Mina lifted her nose. She actually tilted her entire head, but it appeared that it was just her nose that lifted that way. She said, "I dislike intrusive women."

Tom asked, "How about intrusive men?"

"It depends."

Both men laughed. They exchanged quick glances and just laughed softly and with great humor.

Mina tilted her head fifty-five different ways. Then she said, "It's time for bed, husband—"

Tom looked disgusted as he said, "She thinks you're too old for an all-nighter?"

But Mina only raised her eyebrows slightly as she finished her sentence, "—let the child go to bed."

Both men laughed. Tom, by then, was old enough not to be indignant. He rose from his chair and put his hand on his dad's shoulder. "I appreciate the visit."

John put his hand on top of his son's. "Anytime."

Tom told his mother, "You sure knew how to pick the daddy for your kids."

She lifted a hand to her forehead and responded, "It was a trial!"

John shook his head. "Yeah. There were about a dozen of us floating around her waiting for her to decide."

"A *dozen!* Mama, were you a loose woman?"

She lifted her eyebrows and tilted up her chin as the men laughed softly. She said the obvious. "A—careful chooser."

Tom asked, "How come daddy won out?"

Mina looked over at her husband and smiled softly. "He is the best."

But John adjusted his body in the chair and corrected his wife, "I fought every single one. I was always bruised or limping or in an arm sling. My hand knuckles never had the time to heal. She's really something.''

Tom said, ''That's why I want…somebody who's special.''

His daddy replied with a nod, ''We're all that-away. I was lucky.''

Mrs. Keeper leaned over and kissed her son's forehead. ''Sleep well.''

John rose and hugged his son. ''This was a good visit. We'll go to the first game and watch who's best.''

Tom sighed. ''Yeah…it'll be the Cubs, just wait.''

His daddy lifted a stopping hand and turned his head a little as he said very seriously, ''We'll wait and see.''

Mina shook her head once and sighed.

Tom laughed.

They were still talking as they exited the room. It was late. They whispered. The parents went on off down the hall. John put an arm around his wife and she leaned her head on the front of his shoulder. They were talking and their laughs were silenced enough.

Tom stood and watched them. They didn't even turn at their door and wave. They'd forgotten him. He smiled, so amused. It would be like that for him at that age. *His* wife would be that way.

He went along to Ellen's door and stood with his hands in his pockets as he tried to look through the solid door and see her in bed and asleep. No, she was awake and pacing, she was so hungry for his body. Yeah. Sure.

What man on any ranch needed additional exercises?

He went upstairs, stripped and put on running clothes and shoes. Those clothes gave him room and he wasn't conscious of their being on him. And the shoes were high and supported his ankles on that uneven ground.

He wore a billed cap and he wore gloves. Nobody knew what he'd run into at night when he ran. Dogs especially. He'd take a couple with him. He'd have trouble convincing his favorite to hussle around and get out of the house.

Well, how long had it been since Tom went out jogging at night? He picked up a flashlight. Might as well see where he was going.

Coyotes.

Yeah.

He took a pistol and settled the gun belt on his hips. It was only then he thought he might rattle the watch. He stripped, put on swimming trunks and went out to the pool.

Not too many TEXANS thought it was rash to swim at that time of the year. The weather was okay. He dived in. The dogs came along and got on the chairs to watch. They thought he was crazy and needed their attention and protection.

Flashlights came along. The night crew flashed them on Tom and asked, "What the *hell* are you doing?"

Tom reached the end of the pool and lifted the goggles from his face. He said, "How come you guys aren't swimming?"

One of the crew said, "Oh, hell, it's Tom. He's gone nuts."

Tom protested, "I hardly *ever* get the time to swim! I work my tail off."

The two crewmen said nothing more because Tom had started to swim again and couldn't hear them anyway. They shook their heads and went on off. One said to the other, "Thank God Fibee married me. I don't have to swim at night anymore."

"You did that, too?"

The one sighed. "The things a man has to do because of women is mind-boggling. Mostly running— not away from most of them, but just to be able to *sleep!* I remember—" And they walked on off around a corner.

Everybody soon knew that Tom was interested in one of the guests. A woman. They watched him slyly and smiled. They also tried to help him. They'd seat the two side by side at the table. They'd get him to help her with something. She was surprised when he was there with a car when she was committed by Lu who had enlisted her in giving Angela a fifteen-minute breather twice a day.

Those first days were difficult for Ellen. It wasn't the kids, but her stamina. She survived. It had been Lu who took Ellen in a car for that break. But it was soon Tom. It was Tom most of the time, but he was not always available. His ranch responsibilities intruded. Lu Parsons was so amused by him.

Oddly enough, it took Ellen quite a while before she actually understood that Tom wasn't a lolling, indifferent heir who had no commitments. The next time the bull got trapped in the wash, Tom took Ellen and Angela's kids to at least see what was happening.

Tom loved it that he was escorting Ellen. He took her elbow. But he also lifted the kids and watched out for them. That morning, with Ellen and Tom in control of the kids, Angela had almost an hour of peace.

Ellen told a blank-faced Tom, "You were so kind to let the kids watch the bull being saved."

She thought *that?*

When they brought the kids back, they found Angela asleep. She blinked and pulled herself out of bed. Ellen looked at her with compassion as she said, "Go back to sleep. I'll be here until lunch."

However, Lu told Tom, "Ellen's had enough. Take her back to the Keeper house. I'll handle this."

While Ellen's exhaustion was obvious, she did protest that she needed to help. However, Tom agreed with Lu and said, "Not this time."

He drove Ellen back to the Keepers' house. He took her inside. It was lunchtime. The gong had rung. The two split and hurried to wash their hands and tidy themselves a bit. Then they went to the dining room.

They were almost a tad late, but Mrs. Keeper had delayed lunch until they arrived. That woman knew everything. She was truly a hostess.

For that day, Mrs. Keeper had concealed the side dining room's guest whom she was instructing. It was more important to observe Ellen with her son

Tom. It was very obvious that Tom was zonked. What about Ellen?

Mrs. Keeper watched the young woman when she could. Ellen seemed easy enough. She was tired. She listened to Tom and she smiled. She didn't laugh out loud. But she did listen.

Four

It wasn't but a day or so later that the doorbell rang, and it was an uninvolved Ellen who went to see who was there. Again it was the cat. How had the cat learned to ring the doorbell? *Was* it the cat? Or was it some hilarious person who found that amusing?

The cat came into the house past Ellen. It had a high tail and casual walk as if he owned the place, and Ellen was a tolerant slave. However, Ellen didn't notice the conduct of the cat because she was looking for whoever must have rung the doorbell.

Ellen even went out on the porch. But there was no one but a yard man who was some distance away and raking leaves. It *had* to have been the cat who rang the doorbell. How had it learned to do that?

She went back into the house. There the cat then meowed and indicated that it wouldn't mind a taste of something if it wasn't old but something new and fascinating.

So Ellen led the cat to the kitchen. The crew had just about finished cleaning up after breakfast. She asked, "Does this cat *really* ring the doorbell?"

The crew looked at the cat with some disgruntled tolerance. One man said, "I would guess about five times a day."

One of the women said, "Yep. He thinks we don't recognize him and he is here for his food...each time. If you will notice, he's rather plump."

Ellen inquired, "Then he is a he and the plumpness isn't for a fertile female."

"Correct."

She leaned over the cat and said, "Go out to the far buildings and look for mice."

The cat walked around her without touching her or rubbing against her. He knew a misfit right away. He went over to the crew and looked up pitifully. Instead of a rude meow, it said, "Mew."

Ellen gasped, "How clever!"

One of the crew replied, "It gets worse."

Another put in, "If it gets past time, the cat gets rude and says unspeakable things. You can tell by the manner of his yowls."

Ellen laughed.

The cat turned his head and stunned her with one look.

Unfortunately, Ellen was not stunnable. She just laughed.

The cat made the mistake of switching his tail. He'd revealed he was irritated. Stupid.

One of the crew went to the cat, picked it up and pitched it out the back door.

That made the whole crew laugh. The cat landed gently on all fours. He switched his tail, then he started around to the front door again.

One of the crew told Ellen, "Look outside before you open the door. If it's people out there, it's generally okay. Otherwise, don't open the door at all or the cat gets inside."

With interest that was unusual recently, Ellen asked, "Is he a mouser?"

"We doubt it. He's too lazy."

"Give him a mouse. See what he does with it."

The crew communicated looks with each other in delight.

As Ellen walked through the rooms, she ran into a group that was chatting together. One of the guests—there were *always* guests—asked Ellen, "Would you enjoy a ride? The horses are too lazy, and the Keepers beg us to ride them for the sake of the horses. It gives *them* an outing."

"I would love it." Then she asked cautiously, "How long would the ride be?"

The riders considered each other as they decided, "Lunch," said one.

"About two?" questioned another.

"More like four."

They smiled at Ellen. "How about three hours?"

She smiled back and said, "Not yet. I'll ride later. Have a good time. Check with Mrs. Keeper to be sure you go in the right direction."

One male who was considering Ellen with some vibrant interest said, ''We've been told.''

So Ellen said, ''Hope everything goes your way.''

That one man said, ''I'll be back.''

A couple of others mentioned that they also would be back. The women protested with hilarity. And in the milling and chatter, one told the most interested man something about Keeper.

That made the interested man look again at Ellen. Then he gave Ellen his best smile. He said, ''Save me a dance.''

After the group had left, Ellen sought out and asked the senior Mrs. Keeper, ''Are you giving a dance tonight?''

''Not that I know. Why?''

''One of the men told me to save him a dance tonight.''

''Oh,'' said Mrs. Keeper. ''I see,'' she said. ''Hmmmm.''

''What's that mean?''

''I'll discuss it with Tom.''

Curious, not understanding at all, Ellen asked, ''What…will you discuss…with Tom?''

Mrs. Keeper looked at Ellen and raised her eyebrows. ''The dance.''

Ellen said a nothing, ''Oh.''

Ellen went to her room and stripped. She stood under the shower and relished the feel of the water on her body. She poured shampoo into her hand and lifted her hands to her hair. She washed it carefully for some time.

While she had always been neat and clean, only

recently had she begun to realize she was alive. How strange to have been walking on this planet and suddenly to understand that she was actually there. She was one of the multitude who lived on this unusual, amazing ball, which was loose in that region of the universe.

How strange to understand that she was, indeed, there. So. What was she going to do about it? About being there, in this place for a limited time. What could she do to—help.

Into her mind came the time she gave to Angela. So brief, so helpful. Then she considered the Keepers. The family had lived here for generations. Their house was large. They took in people and cared about them.

They had done that same thing for her.

—and how many others?

A whole lot of the people who came there were friends enjoying a holiday, like those who'd gone riding just a while ago.

Once again, Ellen's thoughts turned to her lost baby. She wondered what she could have done to save the baby. Had she been too emotional when Phillip Clark had left her? He hadn't wanted the baby. Actually, he hadn't wanted her.

That realization made Ellen thoughtful.

Did everyone who blundered believe that there had been a reason for it all? A lesson to be learned? How could such a terrible time be a—lesson, she wondered.

Sent by his quick mother, Tom came into the small

room. He moved slowly, watching her. "Are you all right?"

She almost smiled, she was so glad to see him. Her lips parted in delight and her eyes sparkled. She asked, "Why are you here?"

"Well, Mama said we'd be having a dance to-night, and I wanted to have all your dances. I just thought I ought to get to you as soon as possible before you signed up all the dances with everybody else."

She watched him and her eyes got watery. She said, "No one has asked for a dance."

"Then I get them all?"

She smiled at him. He was such a nice man. She said, "You and your daddy and Jerry who is on the crew?"

"Not Jerry. He's a hundred years old and a tomcat and I'd have to dance along with you two in a three-some and it could be very awkward!"

She laughed so softly.

He was very earnest as he watched her. He licked his smile and protested, "If you laughed at even one of his jokes, that Jerry would be underfoot the whole, entire time. He talks fast and you can't keep up, and he's not a gentleman."

"He isn't? He's always seemed like one."

Tom shook his head as he explained, "Men get strange out on the tableland thisaway. You have to take care of yourself...but since you're so frail, I'll do that for you. I'm a Keeper, you know."

Now that last bit could mean just about anything.

Her eyes sparkled as she watched him, and she didn't say one word.

Tom said, "I get all the dances with you except the two when I dance with Mama and you dance with Daddy. Okay?"

She nodded as she smiled at him.

"I'm glad I got that all straightened out. If anybody tries to get a dance, you just refer him to me. Understand?"

"Yes, sir."

"I like that attitude." Then he breathed rather rashly and he said, "I get a kiss."

She patted her pockets and looked around, but he reached out and just lifted her up against him...and he kissed her.

It was sobering. It was fantastic. It was amazing. It was wonderful!

He shivered. His hands trembled. He breathed oddly.

She asked, "Are you all right?"

"Not yet." Then he looked up at the ceiling as he breathed very carefully.

She looked at the ceiling and frowned. "Is the roof leaking?"

"Not yet."

"Are we going to have a big storm?"

He replied soothingly, "I hope it's all simple and easy, but one never knows."

"Why are you here?"

"I wanted to be sure you know you belong to me."

She looked at Tom in some shock and said, "I don't—"

"Tonight. You do. I'll try to give you some room. Maybe tomorrow or next week sometime."

None of that made any sense to Ellen. She frowned as she tried to understand.

He patted her head and said, "Watch out for boarders."

She decided the Keepers were on a fence and desperate. Earnestly, she said, "I have about $20,000.00 I can get right away."

He turned and looked at her very soberly. He asked, "For…what."

She opened out her hands as she said, "To… help."

He watched her. Then his smile began. He said, "Not this time." And he left.

She watched after him. He was eliminating her as help. Twenty thousand was obviously a drop in the bucket. People were going to *board* with the Keepers. Had they gone belly-up financially? With all the people they took in, that wouldn't be a surprise. What on *earth!*

When Mrs. Keeper appeared on the main floor and in a hurry, Ellen called, "Mrs. Keeper!"

She stopped and turned quickly, "Yes?"

"Tom said you're taking in boarders? I can pay for—"

"He was speaking of ships, my dear, pay no attention." That said, Mina Keeper turned away and started off with long steps.

But Ellen ran after her and said, "What's ha—"

Mrs. Keeper said, "Lu is here to take you to Angela for her breather."

"Oh. Yes. Of course. I'll be back as soon as I can."

Mina waved both hands by her shoulders as she went along off saying, "Don't fret. Everything is under control."

That sounded like the Gulf water was rising and was going to climb up and wash right over the whole, entire land!

As Lu drove her over to Angela's, Ellen told Lu that the Keepers were sinking. "They must have lost money on the stock market?"

Lu replied kindly, "I would doubt that very seriously. It's something else. What all's happened?"

"They are giving a dance tonight and—"

Lu was shocked. "We're not invited! I haven't heard one word!"

"Well, apparently it's spur-of-the-moment. Tom came in just a minute ago and told me I was to save all the dances for him."

"What's going on?"

Ellen put out her hands. "I don't know. Something about sinking the ship. Are they financially on the rocks?"

"Good heavens, no." Lu squinched her eyes. "It's something else. You say Tom came and demanded all the dances with you?"

"Yes. How'd you know?"

Gently, Lu explained, "You just said it. That means Tom is worried some other man is after you."

"Who?"

Lu shrugged. "I have no idea. Don't you know?"

Ellen said, "I really haven't been around men for some time."

Lu mentioned, "You've been around Tom."

"Well, yes, but he's been a very courteous host. He's very kind."

Lu slowly slid her eyes over to Ellen in startled understanding. Ellen was a winkie-dink. Not bright. Well, not so with males. How hilarious.

When the time came, Ellen did dress. As usual, she put on her underwear inside out. She did it so that the seams would not be against her fragile skin. And it occurred to her that if Tom should ever strip off her clothing, he would be shocked that she wore her underwear seam side out.

That made her fret a bit. Then she decided she'd tell him ahead of time. Maybe. How in this *world* could she mention casually, "I wear my underwear inside out because of the seams."

Tom would think she was weird. He could be amused or he could reject her. Either way, her underwear would stay inside out. It would take an uncouth man to snub a woman because of seams. It would be a—test. Yes.

She wondered just when he would get to that— uh—debate?

Then she found she was rather startled with herself. She was cured of the man she'd thought was her man for all the rest of her life. Phillip obviously hadn't thought so. He'd only wanted a woman. A reasonable woman. One who was available.

But she'd carelessly gotten pregnant. *She?* No! She recalled clearly saying that having unprotected sex at that time was chancy. Phillip had paid no attention and just stripped her down and...used her.

Ellen put her hand on her empty stomach and a big tear came down her cheek. Poor little almost baby. As soon as its daddy heard there would be a child, he'd left.

The fact that Phillip had left was a telling thing. He was responsible but he'd quickly ducked out. What a bastard the father of her child was.

Actually, the father leaving was, for her, A Great Escape.

How foolishly she'd suffered for losing him. And how she regretted losing the poor little baby.

That night, as the dinner began, the especially interested man who'd asked for her partnership was intense. His name was Harold and they called him Harry. His eyes sparkled and he smiled great. As Ellen recalled, so had the last man she'd thought she'd loved.

Ellen was courteous, but after the dinner was finished, she didn't join the coaxing group nor did she encourage any man. She declined dancing just before Tom Keeper came to grab her hand. He was keyed, his breathing fast and a little loud. He said, "My God, I didn't think I'd get here in time."

She looked him over quickly and he was not limping or bandaged. So she grinned at him. Then she laughed softly as he watched her soberly. She said, "You're here."

"Can I kiss you in front of all these people?"

She blushed and laughed and barely shook her head. "That would be scandalous."

He was holding her hand. He glanced around. "Nobody's looking, kiss me."

She laughed that soft way again and her eyes danced. She said, "Behave."

Looking around, possessively holding her hand, he said, "How should I behave? Wickedly? Aggressively?"

"No. Like a gentleman."

"I've forgotten how—gentlemen—act."

"They are couth."

In shock, Tom exclaimed, "They've lost a tooth?"
She giggled.

He smiled and looked at her with eyes that sparkled with life. He then saw only her. He was intense.

She chided, "Settle down."

He scoffed, "Dreamer. How could I do something like that?"

"Hush."

"If you'd come stay with me a night in my bed, I might be a trifle more calm—for a while."

She repeated, "Hush."

He went on, "—for maybe an hour or so. You'd have to keep helping me."

"You are shocking."

He smiled at her. "I'm not shocking. I'm hungry."

She was serious. "The crew has left. The buffet is open, let's go over there."

He started saying, "—uhhhhhh. My hunger is not for food."

"The only reason I came to this party, given by your mother and father, is that I thought *you* could be normal. Here, you're just like every other hunting male."

"No, I'm different."

She hesitantly inquired, "I—probably—should not ask, but in what way are *you* different?"

"I've been careful. Up until now, I've been just as careful as a dog in a strange house who figures he ought not get on the sofa—as yet."

She nodded. "Don't get on the sofa."

"Damn."

"If you can't be normal and subtle, you ought to go hom— Well, you live here, but you're acting just like the other guys."

"Oh? What have they done?"

"Nothing. You came along at just the right time, but you're no different than they!"

He asked rigidly, "The guys been hustling you?"

She had to laugh, but it was not a cheerful one.

In a hostile way, he urged, "Have they? I'll run them out of here."

"How come you knew immediately that they'd been hustling me?"

"They *did* that?"

"Hush! You're exactly like them."

He dismissed the parallel. He told her, "I'm not

like them. I've been courting you for days and days. They've only just gotten here."

She tilted her head. She asked softly, "What's the difference?"

His eyes came down to her and he watched her. "I can see that it's going to take longer than I figured. You're a holdout."

She thought of her recently past life and the lost lover, then the lost baby. She looked away. Was it ever different?

Tom asked, "Where did you go? You've left me."

"I think I'll see if there's something I like on the buffet. Excuse me."

"I'm your host."

She looked soberly at Tom. "You're one of the hosts. You need to mingle." She smiled lightly. "I'll be around." And she turned to leave.

He caught her arm. "Where you going?"

She looked up at him soberly. "I'll see if your mother needs any help."

Tom told her sober faced, "I haven't gotten to tell you that you're the most beautiful woman here. I've looked at them all."

She tilted her head and looked around. She looked up at Tom and said, "I think you've missed some jewels. Look again." And she went on off.

Ellen didn't dance with anyone. She found several places she could work. The crew allowed it. They were puzzled but figured that way she could do as she chose. She obviously didn't want to dance. She had made that clear. She was kind but final with every man who asked.

Mina observed Ellen and frowned at the pacing Tom who ignored everyone else. He watched and intruded to help with Ellen. She turned her back on him. They'd had a fight? How? Over what on this earth? How stupid of Tom.

John Keeper found a quick time when he asked his son, "*Now* what've you done?"

"Hell, who knows?"

That was in passing. Tom didn't stop and discuss the problem. He was busy keeping track of Ellen.

John thought if Tom lost *this* one, he and Mina would probably disown their child. But just thinking the age of their baby, John began to suffer with his son. He went to Tom and urged, "Let me help."

Tom looked at his dad and said, "It'll be okay. She's had a bad time."

Tom went on off, leaving his daddy standing with his mouth open.

Mina came along and asked, "Catching flies?" Women *never* understand men.

John said, "Our youngest son is in pain."

"That happens. Let him solve it."

"How can you be that blunt." He frowned at his wife.

She shrugged and her eyes were full of pain. "There is no way we can interfere. Leave him alone for now. Find ways to be with him after tonight."

"How could she ignore him? He broke his *neck*, just about, to get here."

"She's been through enough before this. She's been scalded and is careful of anything hot. He'll have to convince her he's kind and gentle and... caring.''

"Did you tell Tom that?"

Mina replied, "Two days ago."

John sighed, "Well, hell."

"I *had* to tell him!"

"No, no. I didn't mean you. I just question real life. Nothing works out."

Mina smiled. "Don't get glum. It'll be okay."

"Now, how do you know that?"

Mina groaned and said, "My bones."

"What's the matter?"

She looked at him unkindly and complained, "*All* of the kids take after *your* side of the family!" And with that urgent information, she just walked on off.

A young woman came over and smiled at John. "Dance with me."

John smiled but he thought: How come no man's dancing with this little girl. Actually, she was listed as a woman.

John took the young thing out onto the cleared floor and they looked at each other and chatted. Who should come along with a patient look but his wife and another older man...who couldn't dance.

John said to the man, "Switch." And he released the young woman and took his wife to himself. She said, "Thank you, John."

"I've done many things to help you out. Don't forget them and give me the cold shoulder. I'm fragile."

Mina lifted her eyebrows and questioned, "Fragile?"

"Yep. I need care and consideration. I'm very sensitive."

Mina said drolly, "I hadn't realized that."

"When we get to go to our room finally, I'll tell you exactly what all you need to know about me."

With unpardonable drollness, his wife said, "I'm trembling in anticipation."

"Any smart woman would know and feel thataway." He did a perfect dip and looked at his wife with a sober face.

She began to smile.

"Don't smile. I'm really ticked."

Mina replied, "Fortunately, I'm rather tolerant tonight."

"Who's ticked you?" Then before she could say anything, he added, "—besides me?"

"Ellen."

"Be kind. She's had a hell of a life."

"Most women do. They mostly manage."

John frowned. "You? Are you saying your life has been hell? How?"

"To live with you…hush…I'm replying. To live with you clear out here on the tableland has been a real strain for me. I've survived because you are tolerable."

"Only…tolerable?" He leaned his head back and frowned down at her.

"You are why I am out in this neck of the woods. You start turning difficult and I leave here really fast."

"I'll be more careful."

Mina was somewhat droll. "That would be wise."

"We're a team."

She clarified his words, "You listen and let me handle—whatever."

"Yeah." He nodded. "That's about right. But the problem with me taking over and smoothing things out is that I can't do it like you do. You're so smooth. You solve anything when I'm still tearing my hair."

"If you just paid attention, you'd learn to do it all yourself."

He frowned. "It's easier when I just turn it all over to you and forget it."

"Yes." She sighed and lay her head on his shoulder.

"I like it when you do that."

"You're a rock."

"Stupid?"

"Supportive."

He hugged her to him. "I love you, Mina."

"Thank God you do."

"Why do you say that?"

"If you didn't love me, I'd probably have to go live with one of my sisters."

"You'd have all your money."

"I'd be lonely."

"You only stay here to keep from being lonely?"

"I stay here because this is where *you* want to be."

"Yeah. I love it here."

She said, "I love you."

His eyes got leaky and he smiled. He said, "That may very well be something we share."

"We'll see."

The music stopped.

They parted just a tad. They looked at each other seriously. He smiled, and she said, "Don't ever leave me."

They ignored everyone else. He then said, "The only way I could ever leave you is if I died."

She responded immediately, "Don't do that."

He hugged her.

Then they began to hear the people around them teasing and asking and laughing.

How strange that people are surprised by those who love each other. Such shared love is that rare.

Ellen had noticed the Keepers' intense and serious exchange and their sweet shared hug. Her face was serious. She'd never had such a relationship.

Tom came to her and took her cold hand in his. He didn't say anything, he just held her hand.

She looked up at him, and she found that he was watching her very seriously.

He told her, "This next dance is mine."

She replied, "Okay."

He said, "You're supposed to say, 'Thank you, sir.'"

"No. The thank you is what you say. I just nod."

Even their sassy exchange had been caused by watching the senior Keepers. The two had influenced the entire room. They generally did. Mina was special. But then, so was her husband. John was very kind. That's why they had the place they did. But it was Mina who never would let anyone be fired. She always restructured them and found them a niche they could handle.

Five

It was rather late when the party broke up. That was because the Keepers' parties were always such fun. They made it easy for the others to enjoy the time. The only two who weren't in sync were Tom and Ellen.

He asked her, "What's changed your mind? It wasn't me. I wasn't around, so it must have been a comment by someone else and about me."

"No." She put her hand on his arm and said, "It's just me. Leave me be. You're better off that way." Then she leaned up and kissed his chin, but she was gone before he could control his surprise and get hold of her.

Ellen leaving Tom that way harmed his view of himself. He'd thought he'd really had a chance with her. What had changed her mind? She was only one of the slew of women who had abandoned him. And he blamed himself.

But he didn't know what he could have done that had cooled her so fast. He went to his room and stripped off his clothes.

What had happened during the party? Well, everybody else had had a great time. It had been noisy and filled with laughter.

What had happened with Ellen?

Tom's mind went over everything he could think of to find out. He had no clue. She'd been okay when he'd asked for all the dances. What had botched that? Who had said what to her that had ruined everything? He *knew* it was not his parents.

Who, then.

He went over all the people there. None was an enemy, snide or sly. They were good people.

He finished putting on his jogging clothes and again went out into the night. He had a path he could follow that was boring as all hell, but he could follow it without thinking about it at all.

The night men called to him and laughed and some even jogged alongside him for a while. Night at a silent place was boring. No outbursts or problems. They were all grateful to be bored.

However, no one forgot that there was the shot horse that had been killed the year before. The horse had been under the fence-snipper Andrew Parsons' leg. The horse had been out beyond for a couple of days. It had happened on far Keeper land. Andrew's dog had found Tom at a rill. The dog had been so dehydrated that Tom had been careful of the dog who was leery of the man.

It was the pilot Rip who'd flown the dog back along the dog's trail and found Andrew. And it was Rip who'd taken to Andrew's sister, Lu.

Lu's brother, Andrew, was just recently married to a fine woman, and she had changed him amazingly. Who would ever believe that could have happened. Andrew had been such a snob, but he'd adjusted himself to this world, and everything had turned out right.

For them.

But for Tom Keeper, life was getting long in the tooth and frustrating. Here, his attention had been caught by a woman who'd been badly used by a selfish man. How could Tom help her heal so that she could love him? How could he save her from a nothing life? How could he communicate with her?

He'd thought they were going to make it together. What had happened that she'd withdrawn from him? Not just from him but from all people.

When his body began complaining about the jogging, Tom finally went back to the big house. There he went in quietly—and the night man moved so that Tom knew he was being watched. Tom lifted his hand and said, "It's me," as he went up the stairs to his room and stripped off the sweat-soaked garments. Then he went into his bath and stood under the shower.

Ellen had heard Tom's hushed comment to the man patroling that portion of the house. She'd heard Tom go up the stairs very quietly. Then she could faintly hear his showering up on the second floor. She'd looked at her watch. Why was he so late getting to bed? Where had he gone? To whom?

Why did she want to know?

Unless there were too many invited guests, the crew always ate with the Keepers. It was routine. So at breakfast somebody asked, "Who the hell—"

"Heck." Mrs. Keeper replaced the word without looking up.

"—heck was out last night running around and making all the dogs bark!"

It wasn't even a question. He wanted Tom to respond.

Tom said, "I wasn't sleepy." Tom had not only admitted it was he but he communicated his sleeplessness.

Those at the table all laughed.

*Every*body knew Tom Keeper was still frustrated and restless. That's how things went in an isolated place. *Every*body knew *every*thing...just about right away.

The amazing part of it all is that while they teased and laughed, they gave their support. They wobbled Tom's shoulders and chided him. But he knew they were his friends. No one was pleased that he—hurt.

*Every*body watched Ellen. And their ears widened and perked up because it was obvious she was in the worst doldrums a human could find. She was suffering.

They told Tom, "You ought to talk to her. There's

something wrong. She doesn't leave here, she's just drooping around.''

Tom looked for Ellen.

He found her in one of the tiny libraries on the second floor. She looked up at him like a sick animal who is trying to hide away and die.

Tom squatted down and put his hand on the arm of her chair. He said, ''Tell me what's the matter. I can fix anything.'' And he looked at her seriously.

She burst into tears.

That shocked Tom. He didn't quite know what to do—besides calling his mama. He really didn't want his mother there, right then. He wanted to be the hero and figure out—what all else it was—for Ellen.

He bent over and squatted a bit and lifted her against him and went over to another, bigger, rocking chair and sat down with her on his lap.

He shifted around and found a reasonably clean handkerchief. He gave it to her saying, ''Just use this side, it's fairly clean.''

In her crying, she heard him and damned if she didn't laugh and hiccup and blubber and cry some more.

Quietly, softly, he moved them back and forth in that rocking chair. He hugged her to him and said, ''Nothing's that bad. I can handle anything except you finding another man you prefer over me. Did you?''

She shook her head. Her face was in that one side of his handkerchief.

He tucked her head against his shoulder, by his cheek, and rocked back and forth singing, ''Hush little baby, don't you cry..." and there were all the lines he somberly made up that were hilarious.

Men do that sort of thing.

It doesn't solve anything, but it makes the crying woman laugh in a watery way.

Finally, she was silent except for her jerking throat.

He asked her, "Gonna let me know which dragon I'm supposed to kill?"

Jerking with the leftover sobs in her throat, she shook her head. But she stayed on his lap and she was against him. Just beneath her bottom, Tom's pants were staunch.

Tom said, "You gotta know I'm your knight... although I don't have any shiny armor. I can solve anything. What made you cry like that? It boggles me to have you unhappy."

"I'll be okay."

"Did anyone say anything to you that caused this?"

"No."

"You just like to cry and upset me?"

She shook her head.

"Would you hold me on your lap if I cried?"

She gulped and choked laughing.

"You don't *want* to hold me on your lap?"

She managed to get out, "You're too big for me."

"Just your lap." He hastened to smooth that out. "I'm taller than you, but my parts aren't humongous." His hand completely covered her small hand.

She understood what he was saying because she blushed during her wobbly laugh. She said, "I have no idea why I'm carrying on this way. I beg your pardon.''

"You've had a hard time. You're eating better. You're nice to hold. You're gonna be okay.''

"How do you know that?''

He was surprised. "I asked the top vet who takes care of all the critters around and about, and *he* said that you'll be—hush—okay. Now you're not *listening*. Creatures are creatures, no matter—listen to me—quit laughing thataway. You're gonna be okay.''

She lay across his chest with her bottom on his susceptible lap. She watched him. Her throat and nose jerked and sniffled now and then. She said, "You're so kind.''

"Because I love you? Yeah. But, honey, I'd hold you if you were ninety years old. I can't stand to see anybody cry. You should have seen Bud when his little girl died. He was so frantic. It took a bunch of us to hold him steady. We all talked at the same time. He didn't hear a one of us. He just was *frantic!* We didn't know what to do.

"Then Mama came out and she sat and held his hand. She asked him questions. Being a gentleman, he had to reply. He did. And she gently got him calm. He loves her. She got him through it.''

Very softly, he asked Ellen, "Should I go get my mama to help you?''

"I'll be okay.''

"Sometimes it's easiest to talk to somebody. Like the Catholics do with their confessions. Do you feel the need to spill your guts? I've seen everything. Tell me and I'll help you with whatever it is that's riding you.''

There was a pause, then she said searchingly, "I've been—lost—in a way. I've not really wanted to be a part of this world. You and your family have been so kind to me. I haven't realized how many people come to you."

He discarded being involved. He told her, "My mama. She *always* knows what to do with just about *any*thing. Go to her if you can't communicate with me. I'd help. You could tell me anything. Are you a crook?"

She laughed in soggy way, "No."

"You killed anybody?"

"Good heavens, *no!*"

"You stole a man from another woman?"

She shook her head.

"Well, then, I'm stymied. What *have* you done?"

"My baby died."

He hadn't forgotten that.

She gulped with her emotion.

He said softly, "Yeah." She wanted to talk. Could he be calm enough to listen? He said, "That's tough. He wasn't ready to be born. I've forgotten how old he was?"

"She was but six months inside me."

He altered the baby's I.D. "Did you get to see her?"

"No. Not really. She was still quite little."

"Sometimes little kids aren't growing as they ought. She probably wasn't meant to be."

"That's what the doctor said."

"Then you ought to let her go. It's tough, but something was wrong. She preferred to pass on living. She was probably smart."

"That's what they told me."

"Is that when the...person...left you?" Tom just couldn't say "man" for such a nasty wimp.

"He'd left sometime before then. When I said I wouldn't abort the baby."

Tom said with conviction, "You were lucky to get away from him...you aren't yearning for the bastard, are you?"

"No. The baby."

"After we're married—"

"I don't think I could ever marry anyone."

"Well, we'll wait and see. I'm a very willing husband. You can hang around and decide. If you just *can't* stand me, I'll probably become a hermit."

"No."

He drew a deep breath. But he couldn't think of anything else to say to her about the baby. So he said, "You hungry? Emotion always makes me feel starved. I need a peanut butter sandwich and a glass of milk. How about you?"

"No."

"Come to the kitchen and watch me put together the *best* sandwich you'll ever see. And I just—might—give you—a—quarter of it. Hah! Fooled you there, didn't I?"

She shook her head a bit. "I don't want anything to eat."

"Well, I don't mind that a-tall. But don't you

come around begging for part of mine after I've made it. Hear?''

She replied, "I hear. But I don't believe my stomach can watch you eat. I might gag.''

He considered her. Then he suggested, "You can sit backwards and still *talk* to me! You can't just go on off to bed and—desert—me—leaving me all alone in this house.''

She said kindly and gently, "There are people everywhere around. You stumble over them. Your mother is probably training them for a better life. You are all strange people. You're a very nice man.''

He agreed instantly, "I'm darling. You need to know that. I've never before admitted to a woman that I am—darling—but you just need to know that I am. I'm also precious.''

She watched him and murmured softly, "I see.''

"I'm glad you do. It helps if you understand that and then you won't be startled when you realize it's true.''

Her laugh was soggy. That was the only way to describe it.

She was on his lap and had been for some time. He put his arms under her shoulders and knees and stood up!

She gasped, clutching him. She managed, "How'd you *do* that!''

"Well, hell, I guess I'll have to tell you the truth, I'm magic. I can do all sorts of things.''

"Like—?''

"I can cook and eat and make beds, and dust and vacuum.''

"No!"

"Yep. Mamma didn't let a one of us escape being a cleaner-upper. She was vigorous about it. She's normally a director. We flinch and try to sneak away."

She asked, "Do you ever get away?"

He nodded. "On occasion."

"Mostly—not?"

He had carried her down the hall and across the rooms to the kitchen door. No one was anywhere around. Mina saw to it, and she, too, had vanished.

In the empty kitchen, Tom put Ellen on a chair. "Now watch. If I do something wrong, you may mention it—once—and you can taste what I've made me if you behave."

"Yes."

But instead of a sandwich, Tom made pancakes. He flipped them and most of the time he caught them. The others were retrieved and discarded quite casually as he said, "Not balanced" or "Too heavy" or "A discard."

She bit her lips and her eyes danced. She even ate one of the pancakes! But her eyes couldn't stay open. She was exhausted. So he abandoned his plate, scooped her gently into his arms and carried her to her room.

Her arms were around his shoulders and she couldn't keep her eyes from shutting. Her head was unbalanced, so he shifted her and her head lay on the front of his shoulder against his throat.

When they arrived at her room, she did lean to turn the doorknob. His foot again opened the door for her and he took her inside. Tom said, "I can strip you and put you in a nightgown. I've done that for men at the hospital. I've even washed them. I'd be tolerant in doing that for you." The only thing wrong was that his voice got husky.

Ellen said, "Never mind." Her eyes blinked slowly and she moved gradually as if in a dream.

"With all those wet tears, you're soggy. You need a nice, hot shower."

"I'm too tired."

"Either you shower, or I give you a facecloth rubdown with hot water."

"You're being abrasive."

Tom promised, "You'll sleep like a log."

"I would anyway."

"No. I'm an emergency trainee for the medics we have, and I've learned a whole lot about people. You either shower, or I'll give you a rubdown. I would suggest you strip and just lie on the towel on your bed—" his voice was foggy "—and I'll give you a good rubdown."

"Never mind."

"You choose the—shower?" His voice squeaked up in shock.

She sighed with elaborate endurance. "There's no other choice with a man who is a maniac."

"I'm a lover."

She hesitated, and he saw that her eyes looked off to the side in alertness.

He said, "I'm only a lover to a woman who loves me." His voice was low and steady and kind. "I let her decide."

"Oh."

What a nothing response. He turned his back and said, "Loosen what needs it. I can bathe anything."

"I'll shower."

"Well, damn."

She shook her head as she went into her little bath. But she was smiling.

To Tom, just the smile alone was a big leap forward for her. She would make it. Eventually. And his eyes slitted as he thought of giving that bastard Phillip a really serious right punch.

Tom was not a fighter. He'd seldom even needed to chide anyone. And he tried to think if he'd ever before wanted to use his knotted fist to hit a man.

That was a very sober observation. He'd wrestled with his brothers. But that hadn't been serious. And it had been holding and tripping and that sort of thing. Had he *ever* actually hit any other human?

He was thoughtful.

She came from the bathroom into the unlighted bedroom. She wore a silk robe. With the bath light on, the robe was transparent for any practical purposes, and Tom could see the outline of her body. He sighed. That meant he'd have to jog another couple of miles before he slept.

He turned back the bedclothes and watched her discard her robe. That wobbled him considerably, and excited his breathing, but she was wearing white silk pajamas that clung to her skinny body very carefully.

Knowing that, didn't adjust his lecherous body or

his wild mind. Maybe it was a wild sex and a lecherous mind? Whatever. He'd get to add another mile to his jogging. Lucky, lucky him.

He didn't speak aloud. The hot bath shower was just what Ellen had needed. She wasn't even aware of him as a man. She allowed him to pull back the covers and she got into the bed. He covered her gently and minimally. He did not linger.

Exhausted, she began to drift into sleep almost immediately. And she never heard the door open or close. He'd oiled the hinges.

She slept.

He did not.

The various night crews' stints had communicated with one another, and while they'd laughed over Tom being thwarted by a woman, which of them hadn't experienced the exact same thing sometime or the other?

Their laughter was compassionate and the verbal jostling was gentle…for men. They gave Tom all sorts of advice.

He replied, "I tried that" or "I'd never be able to get her that far from mother" or "Don't you guys have anything *else* to think about?"

Life went on. Things happened but nothing was mind-boggling. It was about normal for that many people being underfoot. The cat continued to ring the front doorbell looking for a handout.

What happened? One of the crew caught a mouse. And he put it in a hinged, wire basket used to dunk vegetables.

With the mouse in the basket, that way, they could all keep track of the mouse. You couldn't put a mouse in a drawer, it would get out the side or the back of the drawer. The wire basket was the only place for it. There was no other place it could be...be seen and be alive.

The damned cat came around to the front of the house and rang the doorbell.

The house crew called all the others who were in the stables or in the fields or on horseback. They came inside the back door, and the cat was still ringing the front doorbell. So one of the crew let the cat in.

The cat greeted everybody along the way to the kitchen. The humans knew what was there on the kitchen floor. It was not only something encaged, in the cage was the live mouse!

The women who were a part of the crews were standing on chairs or stools, and everyone was silent as they watched...the cat.

He looked around at all the people and was courteous. But then he saw the wire basket. He became rigidly alert! He froze and watched. Only the tip of his tail was not under complete control. The tail end of the cat flicked minutely with excitement.

One of the guys had the bottoms of his pants tied around his ankles. It was he who opened the cage. Both the cat and mouse waited...not sure.

And Tom Keeper said softly, "Two bucks the cat misses."

Well, from there the human bidders went berserk,

and bet on all kinds of maneuvers and odds and who did what all.

It was hilarious. The bidders *also* watched the cat and mouse. They were very alert. The cat with the mouse, the mouse with the cage he was in and all the people who were *enormous*. It was very quiet.

The mouse was very still.

The cat sat down and watched the mouse. There was no hurry. The mouse wasn't going anywhere.

However, the men who were trading sums and discussing who would win became a tad more vocal. In the bets, it was if the cat would eat the mouse and not just kill it, or if he'd become bored and—leave?

How boring was life to have the possibilities of a mouse and a cat catch such attention!

Several of the women even got off the chairs and one simply left. The men decided to put the mouse in her room. Other women gasped in shock and questioned such action. They were quite hostile.

Men exchanged glances and rolled their eyes a tad as they bit at their smiles.

The mouse became a pet, living in the wire vegetable basket. He was fed. He had the cat's full attention. They sought names for the mouse.

One of the guys warned, "You name him, and the cat gets him, you'll grieve."

Another said, "The cat's no mouser."

The reply was: "Naw, he doesn't know the first thing about what to do to get to the mouse. He'll end up just watching the mouse and wanting to play with it."

Someone squeaked, "Eatin' a mouse is *playing* with it?"

"The cat don't know no better. It's spoiled rotten. We feed it all the time."

One observed, "The mouse's skinny."

Another mentioned, "We got to get him plumped up for the cat."

One of the women exclaimed, "He sings!"

Another woman said, "The mouse is neat and tidy."

The men then offered the women the care of the mouse, but they all declined.

Of course, the men began to tease the women for being scaredy-cats with the mice around and about.

One woman retorted, "That's how come we *have* men around here!"

The men were shocked! "Us?" And, "Why, we never in this world knew that! How come?"

One of the women sassed, "We don't like fooling around with rodents."

"Oh. Then Bob...isn't a...rodent?"

Another male gasped, "Well, I do declare! I thought he was."

Another shook his head and said, "Naw."

A woman's voice butted in with, "On occasion—"

When the laughter quit, and Bob's laughter and blushing was the worst, somebody said, "Let's wiggle the wire basket."

"Yeah!"

All the women yelled, *"Wait!"* as they jumped off

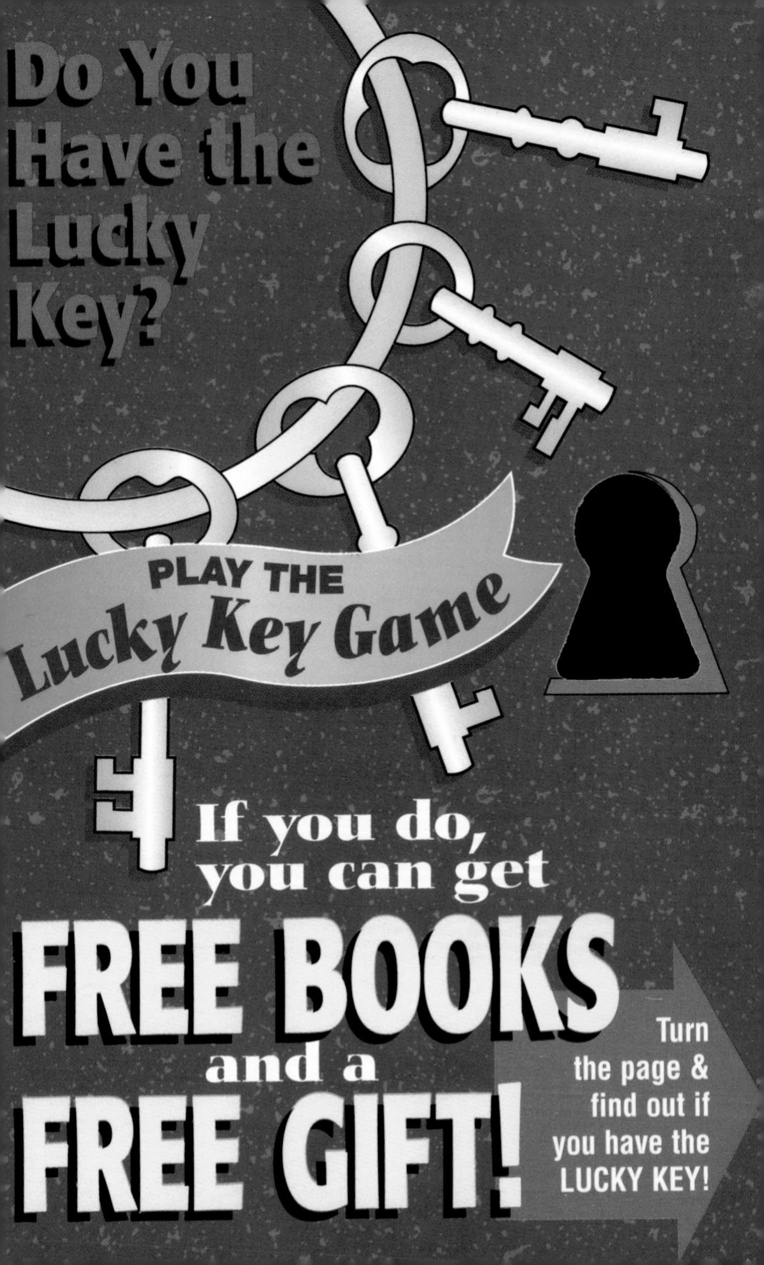
Do You Have the Lucky Key?
PLAY THE
Lucky Key Game
If you do, you can get
FREE BOOKS
and a
FREE GIFT!
Turn the page & find out if you have the LUCKY KEY!

PLAY THE
Lucky Key Game
and get

HOW TO PLAY:

1. With a coin, carefully scratch off gold area at the right. Then check the claim chart to see what we have for you — **FREE BOOKS** and a **FREE GIFT** — **ALL YOURS FREE!**

2. Send back this card and you'll receive brand-new Silhouette Desire® novels. These books have a cover price of $4.25 each, but they are yours to keep absolutely free.

3. There's no catch. You're under no obligation to buy anything. We charge nothing — ZERO — for your first shipment. And you don't have to make any minimum number of purchases — not even one!

4. The fact is thousands of readers enjoy receiving books by mail from the Silhouette Reader Service™ months before they're available in stores. They like the convenience of home delivery and they love our discount prices!

5. We hope that after receiving your free books you'll want to remain a subscriber. But the choice is yours — to continue or cancel, any time at all! So why not take us up on our invitation, with no risk of any kind. You'll be glad you did!

YOURS FREE!
A SURPRISE MYSTERY GIFT

We can't tell you what it is...but we're sure you'll like it! A
FREE GIFT—
just for playing the
LUCKY KEY game!

© 1997 HARLEQUIN ENTERPRISES LTD. ® and TM are trademarks owned by Harlequin Books S.A., used under license.

FREE GIFTS!

NO COST! NO OBLIGATION TO BUY!
NO PURCHASE NECESSARY!

PLAY THE
Lucky Key Game

Scratch gold area with a coin.
Then check below to see the gifts you get!

YES! I have scratched off the gold area. Please send me all the gifts for which I qualify. I understand I am under no obligation to purchase any books, as explained on the back and on the opposite page.

326 SDL CJAC

Name
(PLEASE PRINT CLEARLY)

Address _____ Apt.#

City _____ Prov. _____ Postal Code

🗝🗝🗝🗝 2 free books plus a mystery gift	🗝🗝🗝 1 free book
🗝🗝🗝 2 free books	🗝🗝🗝 Try Again!

Offer limited to one per household and not valid to current Silhouette Desire® subscribers. All orders subject to approval.

(C-SIL-D-09/98)
PRINTED IN U.S.A.

DETACH AND MAIL CARD TODAY!

The Silhouette Reader Service™ — Here's how it works:

Accepting free books places you under no obligation to buy anything. You may keep the books and gift and return the shipping statement marked "cancel." If you do not cancel, about a month later we'll send you 6 additional novels, and bill you just $3.49 each, plus 25¢ delivery per book and GST.* That's the complete price — and compared to cover prices of $4.25 each — quite a bargain! You may cancel at any time, but if you choose to continue, every month we'll send you 6 more books, which you may either purchase at the discount price...or return to us and cancel your subscription.

*Terms and prices subject to change without notice.
Canadian residents will be charged applicable provincial taxes and GST.

If offer card is missing, write to: Silhouette Reader Service, P.O. Box 609, Fort Erie, Ontario L2A 5X3

SILHOUETTE READER SERVICE
PO BOX 609
FORT ERIE ONT
L2A 9Z9

0195619199-L2A5X3-BR01

CDMA
Member

MAIL▶POSTE
Canada Post Corporation/Société canadienne des postes
Postage paid   Port payé
If mailed in Canada   si posté au Canada
Business   Réponse
Reply   d'affaires
0195619199   01

the chairs and left the room, closed the doors and just…vanished.

The men brimmed laughter. They didn't make one hilarious sound. They coughed and blew their noses but they did not let any woman know the men were that amused by them.

The reason they did that was because they wanted something similar to happen again with mice and women but not for a while.

They *said* the mouse escaped. That's what the men said. They opened the top of the lettuce wire holder, and the mouse…just left.

After that, the women walked carefully and looked around on the floor—until one of the men said he'd seen the mouse on a chandelier. That rattled all the women.

The men went along exchanging sly looks and licked grins. Then Bob was in the storage room and a mouse went up the leg of his pants! Talk about *hysteria!* It took five guys to get Bob's pants off and try to find the mouse…which had escaped.

After that, the men were more careful. And they didn't smile and cough as much.

Tom asked Ellen, "You 'scared of mice?"

"I had one as a pet once and—"

He was shocked. "You did?"

She nodded. "The kids came home with me after school so they could see him. He was quite comfortable with a group."

"What happened to him?"

"He had babies."

Tom blinked. Then his grin began. "Who was the daddy?"

"My father was curious, but mother was appalled there'd be *another* mouse around."

"What did you do with the litter?"

"For a while I had all sorts of sudden friends who wanted to help me with the babies. Daddy thought it was cute, but Mother hated all of those mice."

"What happened?"

"Daddy eventually sold the mice to a pet shop."

"Were you sorry?"

She said, "Without the mice, I became ordinary in the eyes of my fellow students."

He tilted his head back a tad and looked at her. He said softly, "I just wonder what sort of stupid students you had to cope with."

She looked at him differently.

Six

As the days passed, Ellen's emotional base began to gradually heal. She didn't offer any comment or criticism or advice, but she listened. She became interested. She smiled.

It took Tom a while, but he realized that the whole, entire crew—male and female—did whatever they could to garner Ellen's attention. Especially, her smile.

When a man is trying for a woman, he'll always notice if other people are vying for her attention. And women! That was interesting. They wanted to be friends with Ellen.

Men's approach was mostly different. They wanted her admiration. Even the happily married ones.

But Tom realized the women were including Ellen

gradually. They liked her. It wasn't something Tom's mother had initiated— Or was it?

Who could figure out Tom's mother? Not Tom.

With all the interest in Ellen and the inclusion of her in whatever, Tom had some problem getting her to himself. He got bolder. He said, "I have something to show you." And the whole entire crew came along!

Once he asked Ellen, "Want to see the new baby chicks?" And he thought he'd spoken low enough that only she heard him, but again the entire batch of people came along.

They went out to one of the barns to see the chirping chicks and the agitated, clucking hens.

Tom told the others, "Take a peek and go on or she'll move the babies." He said that while holding on to Ellen with an unlockable hand. When she tried to indicate that she wanted her arm back, he said to just her, "Be quiet."

A tad indignant, she retorted, "I need that arm!"

"For...what?"

"So's I can move!"

He was indignant in turn as he asked, "Why do you need to move?"

"To see the chicks." She was patient and logical.

"I'll take you in when this invasion is gone. If you recall, I only asked you to come along, not this whole mob of people!"

"You have to be more subtle."

"How!"

"You ask me to see a longhorn or a bluebonnet or something like that?"

He was disgusted. "If I said anything like that, they'd think I was taking you into one of the barn lofts."

"No!" Ellen gasped in shock.

"Yep. They're all of one mind." And he looked off nobly into the distance.

Since Ellen was coming out of it and realizing what was going on around her again, she watched Tom while she bit her lip to stop her smile. He was such a dear person.

He was sexually stretched and hurting. She would give him…ease. She would be kind. That would release him from the need he endured. He could relax. And he would realize she was not for him.

That evening, after dinner, Ellen said it was time for her to go to bed. She turned her big eyes up to Tom and smiled just a tad.

How odd. A sweep of the most amazing thrill went through her body! The rush was so astonishing that it wiped her face blank. It parted her lips, which had turned quite red. Her eyes were odd. Unfocused.

She was so startled and astonished by such a wave of emotion that she faced the fact that she might not have recovered from her grief, after all.

Something was pounding her. Her heart was a little off kilter, her breathing was odd. She felt somewhat strange.

She looked at Tom.

He was looking around as if to find a stretcher for her. But he courteously tugged her along the room and out into the hall. He said to her, "Let's go to my room."

She nodded soberly. It would be quieter at that time of the evening. She could go to her own room after all the people left.

One of the men asked with twinkling eyes and a snide smile, "Where you going?"

Just like that, Tom retorted, "To the library. We have a disagreement."

Ellen had heard. So they weren't going to Tom's room after all? Well...how odd. They were going to a—library? Since there were all those tucked away libraries of varying sizes all over the house, Tom could mean just about *any*thing!

They went to his room.

That was a surprise.

As he closed and locked the door, she said, "I thought—"

—and he pulled her against him and kissed her. He groaned and rubbed his hands possessively over her back in hard holdings. He trembled. His breathing was odd.

She asked, "Are you all right?"

He replied, "Soon, now."

She had had two men in her lifetime. One in college and that had been messy and really awful. Then Phillip had been so careful of her and tender...and quick...and selfish. Now was her third.

Third.

This was Tom Keeper. The third man to know her body.

She didn't resist. She quietly sighed and waited for the coupling with the rough, panting of a hungry male who would use her quickly and roll off to go to sleep.

Tom asked, "You okay?" And he bent over to look into her still face.

"Let's get it over with."

The words had just come out of her mouth. Tom was startled. Even more seriously, he asked, "What's wrong?"

She shrugged.

Carefully, he asked, "Would you rather not?"

"It's okay. Let's get it done."

Now that didn't sound at all eager to Tom. He said, "Whoa, now. Let's back up and look at this. What's the matter?"

"Nothing. I've done this before, as you know. It's no big deal."

His sex about went into a frantic overdrive. But Tom looked seriously at Ellen and asked gently, "What's wrong?"

She flared her eyes in indignation as she retorted in variation, "Let's get it over with."

He stopped her disrobing and picked her up to carry her around. Then his breathing slowed enough so that he could say, "We'll talk."

He sat down on his rocking chair and held her on his berserk lap. Her bottom squashed the rigid Hunter and held him still.

Tom asked, "What's all this about '—getting it over with.'"

"It's quick."

Tom's voice was gentle. "Not…necessarily."

"You mean some men can't do it right away? That would be a bore."

"You don't enjoy sex?"

She moved around and sighed and turned her head about forty different ways. She said, "No. I suppose women don't."

"Why not?"

She was impatient. "Men are awkward or too fast."

Softly, Tom questioned, "Or unknowing or selfish?"

The two words went into Ellen's mind. Unknowing? Selfish? She turned her head and asked, "Do you mean men are stupid?"

"Unknowing. Unaware. Selfish."

"Then—"

"A woman needs love. I love you. I want to please your body. I want to make love *with* you."

"How'd you learn all that." It was not a question. And she was very withdrawn and a tad hostile. "You're really triggered. I can tell from your breathing."

He said, "I love you."

"Balderdash."

He laughed softly. "Where'd you find that word?"

"My grandmother."

"It's a dandy. So you think my love is—balderdash?"

"All men tell a woman they love them when they just want sex."

"And, if there're complications—they want out?"

"Yes." It was a brave, instant response. "Like Phillip."

Tom said, "I guess that I'll have to court you a little more so that you can realize that I love you. And—"

"All men use that word. It isn't true."

Tom sighed. "You know I've been amusing all the house and area men with running at night so that I can sleep?"

"Why."

"Because I haven't gotten into bed with you. I really love you. I've been seriously courting you. Do you want to relieve me now or would you prefer to wait until after we're married?"

"You'd...*marry* me?"

"Why else would I've been paying you all these attentions?"

"You want to be in my bed."

He heard the disgust and rejection. He kept her from leaving his lap. He said, "I love you. I want to be with you. I want to laugh with you and tell you what happens in a day, and I want to hear how your day has gone and what all you've done. And I want to make love to you so that you hold me against you and sigh in contentment."

"Who all's done that with you?"

"My daddy and mama told me those things. It's how their life is. I want our lives to be that way."

She said nothing. But he could see the tears on her lashes as she sighed, sitting there on his lap.

He asked, "Are you a cold woman?"

"Probably."

"Can you warm up enough to like me?"

"I doubt it. I believe sex is probably the worst thing that ever happened to me."

"But you wanted the baby."

"Yes."

"Did you also want the man who gave the baby to you?"

"No."

"Could you ever love me?"

"You're very kind. You sit here and hold me without doing anything to my body except to hold it carefully. When will you decide that you want my body and just—take me?"

"When you ask me to."

She made a rude sound of dismissal.

"Can you stand for me to hold you this way?"

"I'm comfortable."

"You're so tense, none of your muscles are relaxed. You're as stiff as a poker. Why are you that way?"

"I'm waiting for you to pounce on me and take me."

"What if I wait until you want me?"

She shrugged. "I never will. I—dislike—sex. I—don't—want it—at all. You're a good man. You've been kind to me. I will allow you the release. Do you have a condom?"

He tilted back his head and closed his eyes. He breathed through his mouth. He didn't move.

She asked, "What's the matter."

"My body wants you."

"Well—go ahead. I'll let you."

He shook his head.

She shifted restlessly on his lap, which stimulated Hunter quite shockingly.

She said, "You need the release. Go ahead."

"I don't want a—release. I want to make love *with* you."

She burst into tears.

He held her and soothed her. He kissed her wet cheek. He shifted and got out another clean handkerchief and did a lousy job of wiping her tears.

She took the handkerchief and cried into it.

"I've never before *told* a woman I loved her and had her burst out crying thisaway. How come you're crying? Do you dislike me that much?"

She sobbed with her face in her handkerchief covered hands.

He asked, "Why are you crying? You've already rejected me. Does that make you sad? Why?"

With bumpy hiccups and gasping sighs she said, "I suspect you're a fine man."

"Well, I've been told that I'm the best thing that ever came down the pike, and my parents have said that, so it must be true. Do you realize that maybe you ought to look me over again and see how perfect I am?"

"I'm not perfect." She said that in a low, deadly serious voice.

"Well, you may not think so, but you are perfect. I like the way you smile. I love the way you tolerate that damned cat. You pitch in and help, without groaning or looking pitiful. There are a good many things you do that make me proud of you. I love you, Ellen. I have a bad case of you. If you reject me, I'll leave you be, but I'll probably never get over you."

She cried.

He held her sweetly and hushed her, telling her that he understood and she wasn't to cry about him beca—

"What do you mean you 'understand' that I'm crying for *you*, you idiot! I'm crying for *me!*"

He said, "Oh."

That was about all he could think of to say at that time. She boggled him. She was unhappy about—herself? How come?

He asked her, "Now just tell me why the *hell* you're unhappy?"

She bawled.

He became a tad annoyed and said, "You're perfect, you're beautiful, you can walk and talk and nobody notices you doing anything odd either way, what the hell have you to *cry* about?"

She sniffled and used his next clean handkerchief, quite easily taking it from him. She wiped her eyes and she considered his words. She said, "I don't know *why* I'm crying. I suppose it's because I've been so used and don't want to be used again."

"Who all's done that?"

"Two men." She adjusted it, "One young male and a grown man."

"Just that makes you feel…used?"

"Wouldn't *you?*"

"Naw. I'd forget it and go on. You only knew them in a small portion of your life. You give them up and just go on. There's a whole lot out there waiting to be seen. Try it."

"You're asking me to leave here?"

"No. I'm suggesting you look around and see all the other people who have lived and learned. You need the learning part."

"Go back to school?"

"Naw. See the world. Watch how people live. How they manage. What they do. How they react. You have a lot to learn. To accept. To understand."

"Then...help me. I don't know how to get started."

He was silent as he took a deep and enduring breath.

She asked, "Does that kind of breath mean you're irritated with me?"

"Don't be so sure you're the only subject on hand. I'm letting you go. It is one hell of a gift from me that I'll let you roam loose and find out what *life* is all about."

"You're rude."

"You have a long way to go before you understand people."

She was indignant. "Of all things, I do understand people."

"Understanding will be your first challenge. We'll start with the women who live out this way and what they do."

"I've helped give Angela a fifteen-minute break so she can breathe twice a day and not have the kids all over her."

"Glory be."

"That doesn't sound at all kind. What are you saying?"

"Why don't you take them away for a day and give her a real break?"

"No one mentioned that to me."

"As I recall." He drawled that out somewhat. "You were very fragile when they limited it to just fifteen minutes."

She lifted her head thoughtfully. "Your mama was being kind to me."

"To you both. With the fifteen minutes, not only did Angela get a breather, but you got the good feeling of helping...for fifteen minutes."

"What would your mama give me for help—now?"

"Let's ask her."

Ellen went over to the hospital and changed beds and emptied pans and gathered discarded clothes. She was taught what was washed and what was burned.

As she went along, the time expanded from a couple of hours to half a day...to a full day. For Ellen, it was satisfying. Oddly enough, she felt as if she was—healing. And it was clean beds, clean clothes, organization, neatness.

She still stayed at the Keepers. She told Tom what was going on and who was involved. She did not gossip. At all. She told the things that were done and why.

Ellen had never before done anything important. Nothing that helped. It was invigorating that she could *see* what she had done and how she had—helped.

Tom told her, "There are other people who need help...in another way."

She asked, "Like Angela? I've worried about her."

"Lu is helping her out."

"Good for Lu."

Tom expanded Ellen's knowledge. "Lu was already sitting with the Beckers' kids before she dragged you into helping."

"Lu was? Why, how wonderful! I wondered why she was visiting with Angela while I was taking care of her kids."

"That way, Angela could sit, relax, and talk with an adult." Tom then added very gently, "Lu just about always went over and fixed lunch and fed the kids at that time while she and Angela talked."

"Lu is a jewel."

Tom told her, "So are you. You were so fragile, and you felt such sympathy for Angela. You went over there when you could hardly walk."

Ellen's eyes lowered as she glanced aside but she admitted, "I thought of my baby when I held hers."

Gently, he promised, "We'll have kids one way or another. And you can hold them all."

She laughed. She did. She was so joyous that Tom's eyes got wet. She didn't actually notice.

To her, Tom was a rock. Rocks don't have emotions. Rocks are around to support the fragile needs of others. They're used to build safe places. She felt secure knowing the rock who was Tom would keep her secure and safe.

Who would make life secure and safe for Tom?

Ellen spent her time scrubbing and mopping and straightening and ironing. It was all a learning experience. Ellen began to understand one of her friends who complained about her mother making her do so much—stuff—around the house. And the mother had heard and came into the room to explain, "If you don't know how things are done correctly, how can you direct someone else in doing them?"

Mothers always say things just like that, and it's generally years until her children understand. That's when they're teaching their children.

However, Ellen's mother had never taught her children anything. She had married a rich man and decided *her* children would live at the top without getting their hands dirty. How stupid. If you don't know how to do something, how can you teach or correct someone else?

As Ellen worked, she became stronger than she'd ever been. And she was eager to attack anything. Her life was so different! She'd had no idea how busy a body could be. She met so many other people, and they were friendly. The men smiled. The women laughed and shared the gossip.

But their sharing wasn't gossip as such, it was how wrong gossips could *be!* That was the lesson. Never believe what you hear—or see. Even one's own eyes can be wrong because the brain can be wrong, and its analysis isn't altogether correct.

Life is baffling. Fascinating. Fooling. Ellen was gradually learning that. How strange that she had to come clear out there to Mrs. Keeper before she began to heal.

She understood that she had been "ill" for a long time.

It wasn't her mother's fault. She was just so busy with her own group that she hadn't noticed her children. But understanding that something had to be done, her mother had sent Ellen to the Keepers.

Their name. Keeper. Ellen had always thought they just never let things go. They were keepers. Now she was understanding that the Keepers knew how others should keep their lives on track.

It was a thoughtful revelation for someone to understand.

To be in touch with the world in the right way, Ellen watched the Keepers to understand exactly how they did things. That they mixed people. That they listened. That they maneuvered people. That they had the room and patience to allow people the time to understand their own lives.

At the Keepers, Ellen was still hearing about Andrew Parsons. She had met Lu, Andrew's sister. Lu was already a solid woman. Andrew had had a longer time of—evolving.

Then Ellen wondered thoughtfully, did the Keepers keep those odd ball guests around to entertain the crew clear out there on the tableland?

She observed the Keepers. She could do that through Tom. She noted that the senior Keepers really liked each other. They shared temper, love, hilarity and concern. They were a couple.

They also liked their children.

It was only then that Ellen realized her mother had worried over her, and had found this haven for her.

How amazing for Ellen to realize in this frantic time and this peaceful, busy place, that her mother loved her and had found someone who could help her.

Look how long it'd taken Ellen to understand that. So she looked around at all the busy people and began to look beyond herself.

But the interesting part was that she called her parents. She told them what she was doing, and she thanked them for sending her out there. Her mother cried and her daddy blew his nose. "Do you have a cold?" Ellen interrupted herself.

Her daddy said, "I love you."

Her mother said, "Me, too."

When Ellen finally said she'd call again and hung up the phone, she sat thoughtfully.

Tom emerged from another room and watched her carefully. He asked, "You okay?" He'd heard her half of the entire conversation.

She smiled through tears and replied, "I have such nice, kind parents. They love me."

"Anybody would love you."

She considered him. Then she said to Tom, "When I get all straightened out, I do hope you're still around."

"If you keep tabs on me all along the way, you'll be sure I'm waiting."

She tilted her head sassily and smiled smugly. "I'll see to it." She stood up and looked around as if she was just seeing the place. Then she looked at Tom.

He hardly breathed.

She smiled gently. She told him, "I'm glad I know you and your family. You all are especially kind."

His lips parted and he drew in air as if he was a shrinking balloon that needed air especially. His eyes were naked and he watched her.

She smiled.

He told her, "We're not always this lucky on guests. I'm glad you're here. Who's making you do slave work this week?"

She tilted her head and lifted her eyebrows. She said, "I'm holding the creatures who need medical help."

"Wow!"

"I get gloves that are padded. A vest that also covers my throat. And I wear a face mask that is not vulnerable to scratches."

Tom gasped, "Who the *hell* is—"

"I chose to do this." She told him that quite aloofly. "It is an experience at first, then you become very involved with the creature. It is sick or it hurts, and they're being helped."

"It scares me spitless to have you in danger."

She boshed, "Naw. The medics are all very involved with the creatures. They do all the work. All I do is help."

Tom frowned at her. "Don't get hurt."

"I won't. They tell me exactly how to hold which creature, and I do it. They are very pleased with me."

"Double your wages."

Ellen grinned. "I do it free. This is fascinating for me, and it is giving me another look at life."

Tom cautioned, "Be careful."

She guessed, "You don't want a one-eyed woman?"

"I'd take you blind. But I'd hate for you to not see the things that are as awesome as the sun set or the new calf or—"

"Tom—"

"Yeah?"

"You're a good man."

He looked at her with naked eyes. But she just smiled at him and turned away and…was gone.

Tom was fully aware of his mother's busy office and how much she had to do. His daddy was out and about and as involved but in something entirely different from his wife's busy life.

Tom didn't think much about his own life. It was fascinating and busy, but he didn't think of it as being so similar to another's busy day. The—busyness—was equal. What women did was less—different. And until one is hurt or bedridden, how other people do things is not necessarily that interesting.

When the startled horse threw Tom all wrong, no one gasped in shock. They were just glad he wasn't dead.

Of course, hearing Tom was badly hurt, Ellen fainted.

Fortunately, she was at the clinic helping the medical team cope with an ostrich, which is cumbersome at best. Why the grandparents had wanted ostriches on the land was something no one had *ever* understood.

As she was helping to restrain the animal, someone mentioned Tom Keeper was being brought into the clinic. And right then, two men carried Tom in on a stretcher and he was out cold.

That's when Ellen fainted.

The ostrich escaped outside and had to be hunted down later. A really rude bird.

One of the men picked Ellen up and took her outside to lie on a bench 'til she came around.

Inside, Tom began to murmur softly. "Ellen?"

One of the doctors said smoothly, "She's coming." Then he looked at one of the interns stolidly and said, "See what's holding her up."

The intern left and found Ellen lying on a bench. He got some smelling salts and waved it under Ellen's nose.

She shivered and coughed and came to. She looked at the gathering around her and asked, "What happened?" Then she began to get up as she gasped, "Tom!"

The intern said, "Hold still. Just a minute. Don't try yet."

But Ellen got up and staggered around as she said, "Help me get to him."

Seven

White faced and frail, Ellen was staunch in going into the clinic. Two men went with her. They were serious and silent. That scared the very liver out of her. Why were they so solemn?

Ellen thought they were distressed about Tom and were worried about him. Ah, well, men are very strange and woman have to deal with them.

There's nothing else around to substitute for men. The women had looked. Searched. Considered.

Someone led Ellen the few steps to Tom. He was on a gurney. There were a couple of doctors and a nurse all around and over Tom seeing what all was harmed.

One of the doctors glanced up as a pale white looking Ellen floated toward them. The doctor told Ellen, "He'll be okay."

Ellen knew he meant to comfort her. But when Tom gave no response she figured he would be a living disaster.

Ellen said to the doctor, "I can handle this. Do your best."

She said that last so that they would understand she knew exactly how futile any help was, at that time. Tom was out cold. He was a mess. He was dirty and tromped on and probably horse rolled.

Ellen knew what to do and how to do it. She would spend her life taking care of Tom Keeper.

Her mother and father would understand. His parents, Mina and John, would be so grateful. Ellen would devote all her life and time to Tom. Yes.

From the stretcher, Tom said, "Where the hell *is* she?"

He could speak! Who...did he ask for? Who was the—she, Ellen wondered.

A very busy nurse said, "She's here."

Ellen looked around to see what other "she" might also be around there. But the place was mostly packed by male doctors and hands from on the Place. Males. They were not tidy and clean.

Neither was Tom.

Tom said again, "Where is she?"

The nurse was a little impatient, "She's right here!" She looked at Ellen and said rather sharply, "Speak to him!"

Again, Ellen looked around. Then she asked, "Tom?"

Tom groaned, his eyes closed as he said, "Give me your hand. I hurt."

Some male hand took her arm and pushed her right over by Tom! She gasped and was about to protest, but she was where Tom wanted her.

He said, "You're here! I wanted to see you. Hold my hand. I want you here the whole, entire time. If you're with me, I can be brave."

Big, wet tears leaked out of her eyes and ran down her cheeks. She said, "Oh, Tom."

That was all she ever did say. Just "Oh, Tom," and nothing else at all. She didn't comfort him or tell him he'd be okay or *any*thing logical. She just moaned that "Oh, Tom" vocally and apparently that was what he wanted.

He passed out.

But his hand held hers or his fingers went rigid or something like that. And she thought he was dead for sure.

Somebody said quietly, "It worked. Let's get him over to surgery."

Some other medic said to Ellen, "Let go. We'll fix him for you. You don't want to go along."

"Yes."

They took that response wrong and thought she was logical and agreed with them. She was not at all logical nor did she agree with anything at all. She wanted to go with Tom.

Someone took Ellen's arm and led her off. Whoever held her arm, did so in a no-nonsense manner. They put her where they wanted her to be. They directed her quite sternly to be still!

There was an elderly woman who did such and they dumped Ellen with that woman who said,

"Now, honey, I know just how you feel. I've done this so many times that I could *tell you* exactly what is happening when. Your man will be okay. Don't fret."

Ellen said, "Hush."

The old woman looked up in some surprise and asked, "You praying?"

"I want silence."

The old woman replied, "Good. I'll think kind thoughts his way."

"Be quiet."

"Ummmm."

With that last comment, the old woman hadn't spoken but she hadn't been quiet, either. Sometimes people need other people to talk them through something. Ellen did not want *any*one talking.

What Ellen wanted was all in her busy brain as her imagination showed her all *sorts* of pictures of disaster happening and Tom right in the middle of it all.

He would be.

He was that kind of person.

He gave too much of himself in every damned thing that happened around where*ever* he was!

Ellen quarreled with her guardian angel *and* his, and she scolded God and talked to the Devil telling him to get on off, this was a good man.

The whole, entire time was exhausting.

Somebody brought her tea.

Somebody else brought her cookies. She nibbled on one. The tea got cold. It was replaced with a glass of water. She could drink water and did sip it endlessly. The water seemed endless because somebody kept refilling it.

People spoke to her but it wasn't about Tom… And she realized that his parents were there. They were sitting with her. Mina held her hand!

Ellen closed her fingers around Mina's hand so that the older woman would know she was not alone.

Mina said, ''He's okay.''

How like Mina to soothe someone else. Ellen nodded as if she agreed with Tom's mother. Mina would need Ellen to help take care of Tom. How devastating for the parents of such a fine young man. Ellen would help them. She'd stay with them all and do her share.

Time passed in the waiting room, and Ellen lay back and slept without knowing she did that. Her body apparently decided she needed to sleep. How strange a body can be. In control, it can do as it chooses.

She then wondered about Tom's body and what all it was doing, and if it could do…anything at all?

He'd looked so—broken.

With her eyes closed for privacy, she felt the hot tears seep out from under her eyelids and run down her cheeks.

Mina gently blotted Ellen's tears with her useless, tiny, lace handkerchief.

Sleeping helped. It was some time later when sounds came into Ellen's ears. They were ordinary sounds. With her eyes closed, Ellen tried to figure out where she was and why she'd been—out. A wreck? The sounds weren't those of her bedroom not even with the door open into the hall.

She opened her eyes to a carefully softened light. She was in a very small rather tacky room she did not know. She was on a sofa that was staunch and uncomfortable. Mina was watching her.

Ellen licked her lips as she remembered why she was there. She asked Mina, "Are you all right?"

Mina nodded. "Tom is doing very well."

Tears filled Ellen's eyes and spilled over onto her cheeks to take the dried, previous paths down her face and onto her neck. It wasn't something she wanted to happen. She didn't know how to comfort Mina or John. She said questioningly, "I was asleep?"

"Yes. They are still putting Tom together. He was badly hurt."

"Will he live?"

Mina assured her, "Oh, yes. It's just bones and flesh. His vitals are all right."

His vitals. What all in a man is—vital?

She decided it would depend on what a man wanted to do. Did he want to move, to control his life? Get married and have children? Drive a car? Speak? What would a man...choose? To be able to walk? To hear? To do the things he'd always done so carelessly without considering the magic of such a move?

How could Ellen ask such questions to his mother and father? What all did they now know?

Without Ellen's questions, Mina said, "He'll be all right. It'll take a while."

"Do you know what happened to him?"

"Not exactly. Everybody is rather tilted. As far as we know, it was a horse that was spooked."

"Oh."

Mina said, "They aren't sure what did it. But they'd heard a whine of—something. They're going out to see if they can find anything."

Ellen said, "Someone told me Andrew Parsons, the man who clipped the wire fence and invaded Keeper land, spoke about hearing a rush of air just before his horse was shot. It was a bullet from a high-powered rifle."

"Yes."

Ellen asked, "Was it that? Again?"

"We'll find out."

But Ellen pushed, "Was Tom shot or his horse?"

"As we understand it, it was just the sound. Whatever the sound was, there was no bullet in the horse or Tom or in any of the other horses or the men. It was a passing sound. The horse apparently is okay. He did buck and pitched Tom."

Ellen gasped, "Tom was pitched?"

"Yep." That was John Keeper. "And I'm sure Tom is very annoyed that it happened. It's been years since he couldn't stay on a horse that pitched."

Even teary-eyed, Mina Keeper smiled over such.

Ellen drew an unsteady breath. "He's still in surgery?"

"Yes."

Ellen told the Keepers, "I believe I'll go out and walk around. I feel odd."

Mina said, "Go into the lavatory first. You may need to throw up."

"Thank you. I shall." And quite somberly, Ellen got up and walked to the rest room. She washed her face and hands. She looked at herself in the mirror and thought it was a good thing Tom couldn't see her looking like that!

She went outside and found two men following her. They were from the ranch, and Mina had probably told them to watch out for Ellen Simpson. That was a drag. She was adult and able to take care of herself.

Where was she to go—to cry—alone?

There was no such place handy, so she went back inside the tiny hospital—which mostly took care of the place's animals. It must be odd to be a human patient of such doctors.

The doctors could do anything. Not just foolishness, but they could actually fix just about anything. They hadn't found any stumbler as yet. And they didn't seem at all stymied by the shocking harm to Tom.

Ellen wondered who was holding Tom's hand in the operating room when Tom thought he was still holding hers? He was probably completely passed out and didn't know one single thing.

Sitting again in the waiting room, Ellen said to his parents, "He'll be fine."

They smiled at her.

She thought they were relieved that she'd seemed so sure.

She got up and casually paced around, as if she

was simply restless, and not that she was concerned for their son. Of course not. She was just stretching her bones so that she wouldn't cramp any muscles for sitting so long in one place.

She mentioned that casually. It was said quite earnestly so that they could understand. They did and they were courteous about it all.

After a time, one of the surgeons came out and said everything was fine. He actually told that to the Keepers, but he did look and smile at Ellen. She thought the doctor was being kind to the parents of the victim.

She found herself asking, "When can we see him?"

The doctor said, "We're sewing him right now. It will take a while."

They were to wait even longer?

The surgeon said, "He's doing very well. We'll keep Tom close for a while until the anesthetic wears off a bit. When he's taken to his bed, here, you'll be told."

John said to his wife, "We ought to take Ellen back to the Place. It's time."

"Yes."

Ellen put in, "Not right now. I'll come over later."

John said, "The walk will help. Let's go."

John stood up and waited for some response from the recalcitrant although still budding woman.

Mina agreed with her husband. "Charlie will have something special for us. He doesn't often get to choose the menu."

Ellen was trapped. She said, "For a while." For whatever that meant.

They did walk back to the big house. The parents were on either side of Ellen. They guided her quite staunchly. She had no choice.

Ellen didn't eat well. She drank the cocoa that Charlie had made for her.

It had some powder in it that the doctor had suggested. She began to go out like an errant lightbulb. Two of the men volunteered to take her to her room, but all the rest went along. It was Mina who found Ellen's nightclothes. And it was she and two other women who stripped Ellen and slid her into the easy soft silks.

She slept.

She was out of it.

She didn't even dream.

When Ellen awoke, it was the middle of the next morning. She stretched and frowned a bit because she didn't really remember when she'd gotten into bed! She looked around.

A tray was on a small table not far from her bed. On the tray, with the food, there was a field daisy in a narrow vase. The plates were covered to hold the heat.

Now, who had done this? How long ago?

Ellen slid out of bed and went to the bath to wash her face. Returning, she pulled a chair over to the tray and lifted the lids. It was a breakfast for a king— or maybe a queen.

She began tasting the delicacies. It was very like

those tempting trays she'd had earlier in her stay. All were delicious. And as she ate, she wondered if Tom had gotten something similar?

She doubted he'd be allowed to eat this soon after such a horrendous saving of his body. And she thought of all Tom had endured.

Her appetite lessened. She picked very much like the early times when she'd first come there. And she saluted Mina who was so clever with foods.

What disappeared into Ellen was more than what she'd eaten back when Mina and the staff had first torn their hair over her lacking appetite.

Ellen showered and dressed...putting her underwear and bra inside out on her fragile flesh as usual. Then she went out to walk over to the Keeper Place clinic.

As she went inside the building, a nice woman named Freida asked, "What are you here to see?— if it isn't the Keeper boy?" And she smiled.

"How did he do? Is he okay?"

Freida told her, "Go see for yourself. Be quiet. He's asleep. But you can go peek through the door."

Ellen's eyes got soggy. She smiled and said, "Thank you." She thought she did very well and had fooled the old woman.

But Freida immediately called three other women and said, "That darling girl was here for Tom already. And her eyes were all wet."

That made the rounds easily enough. Even Mina heard it...probably second.

Ellen stood in the doorway of Tom's room and watched him. He slept. He snored gently.

The man had had surgery! He was out cold!

But the snore was still soothing. Was he dreaming?

She said softly, "It's I, Ellen."

His snore snorted and he was silent. He moved a little. He'd *heard* her!

She said, "You're okay. Go back to sleep."

He breathed oddly for a few moments, then he slowly relaxed, his breathing deepened and again he snored.

Ellen's eyes were wet. She smiled gently. Even out cold in a *hospital* bed, he could be soothing to a woman! Now that was ridiculous! He was—

Lu came by. Somebody had called her from the hospital to come get this woman who was languishing in Tom's doorway and blocking the nurses.

Lu said, "Come with me." Just like that!

Following the swift steps of Lu right out the door, Ellen asked, "What's wrong?"

Lu said, "Outside of Tom, everything's fine."

Ellen said sadly, "I just…wonder…"

"What is it that makes you…wonder."

"If Tom'll be okay."

"Sure." Lu looked over at Ellen. "Nobody's fooling you. His head's fine. The doctors have had so many challenging problems with the animals that dealing with a human is *easy!*"

"But—"

Lu sighed with some tolerance as she elaborated, "Tom's problem is not his brain or face. He's torn some muscles and broke a couple of bones. He broke one bone in his leg and one in his arm. A couple of his ribs were cracked. He's really okay.''

"With two broken bones *and* cracked ribs?''

"Well, he does have some torn muscles...''

"Good *gravy!* What *else!*''

Lu was alert and serious. "Nothing! He's fine.'' She was thoughtful. "I do believe he broke a little finger on one of his hands.''

That made Ellen burst into tears.

Lu said, "Good heavens! Now what?'' with indignation.

"I'm used up.'' And Ellen blubbered and sobbed and her breaths faltered and wobbled and great big tears spilled from her eyes.

Lu laughed. But it was so gentle and kind as she gathered Ellen to her that there wasn't any way, at all, that Ellen could be offended.

Lu sang "Hush little baby, don't you cry—'' but then she changed the words, and she was salacious and wicked and absolutely hilarious on a man with a broken arm and leg and cracked chest with various torn tendons who made love to a weepy woman.

That made Ellen laugh. It is very difficult to laugh that hard when one is being quiet so she can hear the words. But she was leaking tears and biting her lips to try to listen past her noisy terror.

Lu finished the song and loosened her arms as she looked at the mottled face of the fragile female weeper before her. Lu said, "You do realize Tom Keeper loves you?''

"He's mentioned it.''

Lu advised, "Pay attention.''

With that, Lu just went striding on off across the grass.

With a voice that wasn't at all stable, Ellen called, "Where are you going?"

"To Angela's. You take care of Tom. I'll help Angela."

Lu turned away again.

Ellen just stood there. She watched as Lu efficiently walked away. Lu was disciplined and on time. She'd stopped long enough to soothe Ellen enough. She was sassy. Rip was one very lucky man in having Lu staying with him.

Ellen wondered why the two were only living together and not yet married?

With that fleeting question, Ellen then dismissed the whole caboodle and her attention focused on Tom. Nothing else was of any concern.

Ellen went back to the Keeper house and to her room where she again stripped and crawled into bed. She slept like a log without any pill or shot. Lu had reached her in such a way that she felt Tom was secure.

In times of stress, it's always interesting to know who believes whom...or who all.

Sitting with a sleeping Tom and holding his good hand, Ellen thought about Lu. She was special. She helped everyone.

Ellen decided she would change. She would quit thinking only of herself, and she would help others.

She looked at Tom still sleeping easily. Recovering. Healing. And she thought how fragile people are. In all this world, there are too many people who need help. There are too many people.

Then there were those people who were harmed somehow. Like Tom. How calm were his parents. They understood exactly how much their son was hurt and exactly how serious it could have been. Tom's parents were aware of what he was going through, but they knew he would be all right.

It was Ellen who had thought Tom would be a vegetable, alive and dead at the same time. Mindless.

He was not that. He was all right.

She looked at Tom, still in the false sleep, and she knew how much she loved him. Could he tolerate her? Or was he just eager to find a woman he could be with?

She would see.

Gradually, Tom became more aware of what was around him. He'd had pills for the pain, which had addled his mind somewhat. But Tom knew Ellen was there. Even when she insisted his mother sit with him, Mina accepted that.

However, when Tom opened his eyes, he looked for Ellen. And when his eyes found her in another chair or standing quietly, he smiled at her.

His smiles became more alert. As the days passed, Tom became more like his old self and he spoke. He asked, "Everything okay?"

Then he could say, "Did they find anything out yonder?"

But they had not.

Tom said, "We'll see." That was his response. He

would find out one way or another. He would know who was shooting those humongous bullets and why.

He watched Ellen.

His eyes were kind and gentle. His mouth smiled a tad. He liked looking at her. He told her, "I'm glad you're here."

The men who'd been with him when his horse had thrown him, came to see Tom. They didn't talk about what had happened or why. Not at first.

The men were seriously careful as they went around the Place on horseback or in Jeeps. They tried to find the large bullet that had scared the bejeezus out of Tom's horse. They'd found a rift across the front of the horse's chest.

No wonder the horses had bolted. What would any creature do that was ripped across his chest. Plowing through the hair, the bullet had not touched the horse's flesh. It had simply gone across the horse, there, in a startling manner and it had scared the horse frantic!

The horse hadn't seen whatever it was that had touched its chest and that was what had caused the horse to pitch Tom. None of the other animals had been touched. But they had caught the dismay of their cohort. They, too, had bolted.

The crew tried to figure out where the bullet had come from. North west or south west?

They wondered if somebody was being cute with a humongous barrel. With that long, silent distance for the bullet, did they actually mean to miss the person? Or were they simply too far away. Did they really know the bullet went through Keeper land?

But there had been the actual killing of the horse belonging to Andrew Parsons. The crew had taken time to look back along the trail of the bullet.

After that had happened, all the people were then watching and patrolling around the upper west part of TEXAS. Who would the culprit be? Or would that creature quit and leave them all to wonder as they watched their backs.

And listened.

Eight

Time passed and Tom began to recover. To thank her for sticking by him, Tom decided to give Ellen a dog. It was a grown, serious, trained dog. It considered the female called Ellen with some care. It did not reject her, but it was cautious.

The dog was named Spike.

The name made Ellen sigh rather dramatically.

She bent over and put out the back of her hand to the dog for him to smell as she said, "I shall call you Buddy."

But from the clinic's bed Tom cautioned, "There are about five dogs named Buddy around in this very area. Spike is a tad special. I don't believe there is one dog named Spike in this whole, entire place."

Ellen inquired with lifted eyebrows, "Have you

ever checked? Did you *call* this dog by that name? What does he think of it?''

''It's been his name since birth.''

She laughed with such sparkling, amused eyes.

Tom watched her. He told Ellen, ''If someone you don't like is near you, the dog'll protect you. Just tell him to 'Stay!' and he'll pay attention.''

She said sassily, ''So if you get fresh, all's—''

''Hush. I'm a useless man locked on a bed and powerless.''

She licked her lips and smiled at Tom. Her eyes were... *wicked!*

He told her in a low growl, ''Woman, you cut that out.''

She was indignant! She asked, ''What have I done?'' And she looked as innocent as a newborn.

''When I get out of this damned bed, I'll explain it all to you.''

She tilted back her head and looked at him soberly. Then she asked carefully, ''In what sort of way?''

Being a male, he told her logically, ''You'll like it.''

But his reply made her behave more carefully.

As the days advanced, Tom was lying in bed and recovering with careful—calisthenics. They were called that. Unfortunately, Ellen was there most of the time. She watched. How can a pitiful human man leak tears and object, groan or gasp in front of a *woman?*

Did she leave? No. She watched very earnestly. Then about the third day, she went over to the bed and suggested, "Instead of making him do that, straight out, how about moving his arm this way first?"

He did that slowly with some moxie. It didn't hurt as much.

The exerciser said, "Okay." He added carefully, "At first. But he's gotta learn how to reuse those muscles. They were torn and pulled by the horse's fall."

Without thinking, Ellen closed Tom's hand in hers, and brought it to her cheek. This meant Tom's forearm was pressed into the valley of her nice breasts. His arm wasn't even *on* her breasts but locked between them.

That was enough to silence Tom's protests of pain.

It was later that day when the dog Spike was allowed in Tom's room. Spike had been Tom's dog for hunting...whatever. Birds or men...and the dog loved Tom. He was being very noble in staying with the woman whose name was—uh—Ellen.

The dog went over and laid back his ears very submissively and said a whole lot of things in his throat. He was complaining how *bor*ing life was with a female. He was suggesting that Tom find the female another keeper. Not a Keeper, for Pete's sake, but a dog that was slack enough to tolerate a female woman.

Tom used his good hand and petted the laid-back ears on the dog's head as he said all sorts of subtle things about what a lousy dog Spike was and how useless he was to any normal person.

Spike accepted that joshing as being human humor, but he did sigh with some pathetic drama.

Ellen explained, "The dog is worried that you're still in bed." She was the interpreter. She knew what the dog said.

Spike rolled his eyes with barely tolerated endurance, indicating the backup, the female woman had just made, as to the dog's comments.

Tom licked his lips and bit on a grin. He told the dog, "Be brave. Guard her."

The dog subtly rolled his eyes to communicate what a bore it all was.

With no tolerance at all, Tom said, "Guard."

The dog sighed hugely and went over to the female person and sat nobly beside her.

Tom smiled at the dog.

Ellen thought he was smiling at her. "So, you're feeling better today. You've actually smiled."

That amused Tom even more. He told her quite honestly, "You're so good to see."

She came to the bed and leaned down so that she could kiss his forehead and see if he was feverish. He could look down the neck of her blouse, past her partially covered rounds of her breasts—almost hanging free—clear down to her leedaloo, which is a tummy button or where the angels poked a forming body to see if it was done.

Having Ellen around was sweet torture. There he was in bed...and she was not in it with him.

She could slide out of her clothes and just climb up on him, stuff him in her and give him—release. Yes!

Fortunately, he had a male nurse who stripped him and the bed and managed to tidy everything without any snide remarks.

Tom Keeper's sexual endurance was the gossip of the entire place and the communications shared smiles and exchanged looks of laughter. *Every*body knew that Ellen Simpson was taken with Tom Keeper—and it was mutual.

It was so touching to see the two and watch them. They really didn't pay any attention to anybody else. Actually, that wasn't tolerance. They didn't really *know* anyone *else* was around! They only saw each other.

Food was delivered to them in Tom's room every day. One of those who delivered the food could not resist saying, "I'll feed him." And he'd bite his lower lip to try to cover the laugh.

Every time, Ellen would lift a hand and waggle it as she said earnestly, "I'll do that." And she said, "Never mind, you go ahead and do the other trays. I'll help Tom." She said, "I know how many animals you have to feed. I'll do this one." And she'd smile.

Whoever of the crew who had delivered the meal there, always laughed. And they shared that laughter with Tom, but they shared that plus comments with their cohorts.

It was not unusual that Ellen had no idea how interested the whole, entire outfit treasured all the gossip—about her and Tom. She had no clue that was so.

After all, she'd been working at the clinic, silently holding animals for shots or an exam, cleaning ghastly things up and not complaining at all. She had been a jewel.

They allowed her to take care of Tom. Well, the guys took turns doing the more intimate things.

"I can do that," she said about Tom. "I've done it with the other animals."

That retort made all the rounds with hilarity.

Ellen began to eat her lunch with Tom. The staff was adamant that Tom should feed himself.

She allowed that.

But she ate with him. She had her own tray there. She sat on one chair and held the tray on her lap. The room wasn't big enough for anything else. But she and Tom visited.

He told her when he couldn't get something into his mouth. Then he wanted to be kissed so that his mouth was free and clear. She did that. And they laughed softly. Sharing.

Once Tom wanted a kiss, and she had to unwind the celery from her teeth. He was so amused. He coaxed for a kiss trapped in celery strings.

She allowed that. His tongue was eager to help. He got hyper. She soothed him. She rubbed him. She kissed him yet again.

He slept like a slowly snoring dead man.

The crew *never* allowed *any*one to hang around a human patient at mealtime. After eating, even the animal patients were put to rest. It was quiet time.

Ellen stayed. She felt she was part of the team and not an intruder. The crew tolerated that. They were amused and allowed her to stay.

Tom slept.

She curled up and her heavy eyes closed without her permission. She also slept.

That was reported by the one who gathered the several trays. Most of those in hospital weren't human. They were animals. They were given food quite differently than by tray.

The humans were simply sidelines. And rather something of a nuisance. *Trays!* Baths! Cognizant protests. All that there stuff.

But such a human patient *was* given the same kind attention the animals had.

It wasn't until Tom brought up the question of who had shot that silent, whispering bullet, that such was openly discussed. That he would want to talk about it rattled Ellen.

Tom was healing. He was ready to figure it all out. He wasn't yet able to ride a horse or go out to that area again.

For that, Ellen was very grateful.

But they had put a brace on Tom's leg. They got him up and he could walk somewhat foolishly, with a crutch under his good armpit.

The other arm was in a sling.

To look at Tom in such a position again, standing, scared Ellen's stomach. He would eventually go out and look at where he'd been when he was pitched by his horse.

By then, she knew the horse had bobbled and bucked because the bullet had gone through the hair across the front of the horse's chest. The horse's ears had heard the bullet.

How strange to have an enemy no one could finger. All the people in the area were on watch. None had found any clue at all.

It was a Keeper cousin who came to see Tom with John Keeper along to listen. Klyn was about twenty-seven and he worked on another of the Keeper family ranches, owned by his daddy. Klyn volunteered to go out and about and just look. Search. He'd see if everything else had been checked out.

He was named Franklyn Keeper but he went by the name of Klyn. People are strange. Klyn liked being around and listening. And he was sure he could find out who the devil was being so carelessly dangerous out west of the Keepers.

Klyn was tall enough and looked well made and very male. His features were ordinary but his dark blue eyes were attractive. His lashes were very visible and thick. His eyebrows were also thick.

Klyn's hair was somewhat casual and he could use a haircut, but the wind didn't get his hair in the way of his watching.

He could grow a beard in a week.

But Klyn insisted on doing the search alone. Klyn told a bed-bound Tom, "I understand you wanting to go along, but I'd rather be by myself. I can't wait around for you to heal. With just one, there's less noise. No talking. I have a new, almost nothing saddle that makes no sound at all. Neither horse is shod.''

Klyn soothed the protester, ''I can shoot an arrow very well. I won't make any noise at all. Nothing clicks or creaks or clues us in…the horses or me. Let me try. Leave me be. I'll be in touch.''

John Keeper said, ''Take a cellular phone.''

''Only if you swear you will not contact me.''

John promised, ''It's just to call us if you need help.''

Klyn nodded…once. But he said, ''Leave me be. I would contact you if I need help. But leave me alone. Don't let your curiosity get wild and call me. Okay?''

John promised, ''On our honor.''

As they left Tom, Klyn asked John, ''May I rattle Tom's brain cells?''

''If *he* doesn't mind.''

''May I ask him?''

John said, ''That's about the only way you'll find out. That boy's an independent cuss.''

Klyn smiled. ''I like that kind.''

John added, ''Me, too. He irritates the very hell out of his mother. He never tells her anything.''

Klyn said, ''Finding out will be interesting.''

John said softly, ''Take care of yourself—out there.''

''I will.'' He said that as he stretched. Then he was serious. ''Don't come along trailing me.''

''I promise.'' John took a deep breath. ''You young'uns scare the very hell out of me.''

''No need to fret. Everything'll be all right.''

''Isn't that what's said at night to babies?''

Klyn shrugged. ''I don't yet know that. What I just

said was about what I'd tell any restless adult who is trying to horn in and ride along.''

John was elaborately surprised. "You know all that al*ready?* Well, hell, man, you're supposed to be younger than that.''

"I'm an old soul. I've been killed any number of times. I'm used to it, and I'll see to this or die trying.''

Klyn's daddy's brother said soberly, "Don't do that. I'd suffer.''

Klyn smiled and licked his lips. "I was funning you. You've been sounding just like my...mama. Now, a man your age doesn't want to be called an—old woman—does he?''

Of course, Mina came along in time to hear that and she said, "Why not? Women are what makes this world go 'round.''

Klyn grinned and rubbed his nose. He said, "Yes'um. You're right. Without women, this world would be an empty place.''

Mina tilted back her head and suggested, "When you have the time, remember what you said.''

Klyn laughed softly like a man knows how to do, and he said, "I'll do that.'' Then he took a thumb-first finger hold on his Stetson in a very slight tilt of respect, and he bade them a fine goodbye.

The senior Keepers watched Klyn walk away from them. Mina said, "He's a good boy.''

John chided, "He's a man.''

"Enough of one. He's really still quite young and vulnerable.''

"He's going out to see who's shooting off those

damned big bullets from where the he—heck distance.''

''That should give him something interesting to do. I'll think about him and mentally watch him.''

''Don't get too nosy. Men that age are triggered.''

''Gun crazy.'' She agreed.

''Woman lusting.'' John corrected her.

She sighed by taking in a large breath and her chest went out noticeably.

John knew that because he watched. He said, ''You're acting very theatrically. People will notice.''

''I'm only luring—you.''

''Hah! Let's go to our room before it's time for you to put up your hair in those damned curlers.''

She tilted her head in consideration. ''I could do that.''

They did.

Klyn visited with just Tom and asked all sorts of questions to ''see'' what Tom had seen. They did diagrams of how Tom's horse had moved. Tom slitted his eyes and thought and said, ''Thisaway. About like that. I was watching so's I'd fall on something soft. Grass or sand. There's sand out yonder. Pay attention.''

Klyn listened.

The two talked a long time. Mostly it was Tom in remembering what he saw, of how the sound of the bullet had been. It was little pieces of remembering.

Everyone left them alone. That hadn't been easy for Ellen. Not that she was curious. She just wanted to be with Tom.

It was a long time before Klyn left. The two men

silently shook hands. Tom said, "Watch yourself. Listen. Those bullets are labeled as sounding like something coming through the air. No sound of firing, just the sound of something going through the air."

"I hear you," Klyn said soberly. Then he clasped Tom's good shoulder. "Take care of yourself. We need you around."

Tom said, "You, too."

They looked at each other. Then Klyn left. He moved silently.

That made Tom thoughtful. Klyn just might make it back.

From the house window, John watched as Klyn left the little hospital. If anyone could solve the mystery of those damned bullets, it would be Klyn Keeper. He had always been curious. He had been as a little tad. He always needed to know how and why. If he lived…yeah. That was the rub. How could John ever explain to Klyn's daddy, John's own brother.

John said to Mina, "Pray for him."

"Help me."

"God isn't as tolerant of me as He is of you."

"You're lazy and absentminded."

John was surprised as he considered her words. "I've noticed that very thing!"

Nine

While Cousin Klyn Keeper was searching out west of the area of the intrusive bullets, all the other places were just as busy and so were the other Keepers. They continued to be cautious and careful; but on the ranch, they were busy.

There was the cattle to move, plus the everyday riding the fences and the repair of them. There were their own horses to care for. Along with that, they were aware. Watchful.

Tom Keeper was especially fragile. At the small hospital, it just about killed Ellen to watch as Tom was—exercised.

That's what the therapy ironhanded murderer called what he did to Tom. Exercise? It was torture!

Ellen gasped and her hands moved almost out as she watched simply appalled!

The ironhanded murderer suggested Ellen go visit other creatures that were bored and restless there in the—uh—hospital.

But Ellen said a very brave, "No."

That way, she could be sure the murderer would not actually kill Tom with the maneuvers and bendings and torture!

Tom gasped and squeezed up his face and bit his lip.

The murderer quite roughly suggested, "Tell her it isn't all that bad."

Under strain, Tom replied, "Thisaway, she feels compassion for me and could possibly put her sweet hand on my anguished—forehead."

The murderer questioned, "Where...on your...body?"

Tom said, "I'm not sure."

The murderer snarled, "I can't stay and watch—afterward—and I'll never know what all she did to you!"

Tom raised his eyebrows as he lowered his eyelids and said, "Darn."

Alert and anxious, Ellen said, "Is he threatening you?"

Tom asked the murderer, "Are you?"

The murderer said, "Hel—heck no! I'm just doing what it shows on the page what all he's *supposed* to do! I didn't figure this stuff out!"

The beast was an indignant murderer. He stretched muscles on Tom and his own muscles bulged. To Ellen, it seemed that the murderer was tearing Tom apart!

She moved in agitation. She said, "Stop that!"

Tom told her, "It's okay."

The murderer laughed.

Ellen's eyes were like saucers. She said to Tom, "If you want me to get you help, I'll go do it."

Tom replied, "It's really okay. I'm all right." But then his face screwed up as if—lying on that bed—he'd dropped something weighing one thousand pounds on his foot.

Bravely, she commanded the murderer, "That's enough!"

Tom said, "He still has to do my legs."

A great tear slid out of her eye and began its journey down over her perfect cheek.

The murderer stopped and said to her, "You're upsetting me. Go out and see if you can find a flower for this creep."

Tom agreed. "I do need a flower."

She asked in a shaky voice, "Will you be...all right?"

Nobly sober, Tom said earnestly, "I will survive...even this."

The murderer complained, "Now why did you say that? I'm as careful as I can *be!*"

With watery eyes and biting her lower lip, Ellen went out of the room and almost closed the door. She peeked through the slim crack and watched. The murderer was no different; however, Tom was relaxed and okay.

Hmmmm.

In about ten minutes, Ellen was back with a field flower she'd found. Tom was naked and lying on his stomach. His arm was still encased, as was his opposite leg in its cast.

His eyes were closed. He was lax.

Ellen gasped, "Has he fainted?"

The murderer said, "Naw. He's a comedian."

Tom licked his budding smile.

Ellen said to the murderer. "I may well have misjudged you."

The large, muscled murderer replied with indignation, "Yeah."

With the exercise given him, Tom went out like a light. He slept. Besides keeping his muscles going, he was supposed to sleep after such exercise.

Ellen was still leaking sympathetic tears as she watched Tom sleep. Because he was the victim of the murderer, Tom had been discreetly covered with a sheet...by the murderer.

It was a time for Ellen to watch Tom and think about herself and Tom. He was a good man. He could handle himself. He was careful of her.

She understood how much he wanted her body to calm his, but he was waiting for her to signal him that it would be okay for him—to be with her. To make love with her.

Ellen watched the sleeping man. He wasn't like any man she'd ever known. He didn't just push her down and take her. He did hover. He made it clear to the other males that Ellen Simpson belonged to Tom Keeper.

She hadn't openly, entirely given him that permission—as yet. He waited. He cared about her.

In her core, Ellen's body stirred.

Even in such a slight way as that, she was shocked. Her breathing changed and she was embarrassed. How come no other man had made her feel that way? Respond? Not exactly. He was asleep. Her body didn't mind. Her lust went on. It was…want.

Her eyes were naked and she looked at the sleeping man. Tom Keeper.

She sat and watched Tom who was naked under the sheet. She could strip and just slide into his bed and—under him.

Her breaths were quicker and high in her chest. She licked her lips several times. She became restless.

She took a deep breath and exhaled as if casual about it. She was triggered. She wanted him.

Sex.

The very word had always been distasteful to her. Vulgar. Tawdry. It was in the pit of her stomach. It was none of the things that had always swamped her. Why the change in her acceptance…now?

Why did she lust for Tom when she'd found being with Phillip so distasteful? What was the difference between those two?

She sat in her chair and remembered Phillip.

It didn't take long for Ellen to compare the two men. Phillip was selfish and harsh. He—had—used—her.

Would Tom? Would he come to her like Philip had?

He would take her from the chatting, milling group, and go upstairs and onto someone's made-up bed? Then Phillip was finished like a rabbit. He would leave her there to tidy herself as he went downstairs and off with some of the other guys who'd waited patiently in the car.

Would Tom do that? How could she be sure?

She looked at Tom lying there, under the sheet and asleep. He was lying on his stomach. He was naked under that sheet. He was vulnerable. Why did her body get excited? How come it—wanted—him? Why hadn't her body ever wanted any other man?

That was very sobering to consider.

But her body made her restless. Her breathing was different. She had a tough time trying to control—her—breathing? It seemed loud to her. There in that calm room, why would she feel so noisy and—well—restless?

She wanted to—

She wanted—Tom. She wanted to be under his body with her legs sprawled and her heels on the backs of his knees.

She'd have to be careful of his arm and leg.

Now *why* had *she* thought of *that!* How shocking.

Ellen smiled a tad. She licked her lips and she moved restlessly. She shifted a bit. She breathed oddly. Her puffy lips parted.

She put her hands at the tops of her breasts. She watched Tom avidly. Ellen watched him possessively.

That was a terrible thing to do to a sleeping man. He ought to be warned.

Ellen slid her hands down over her breasts quite slowly. An odd squiggle went in a leisurely circle inside her womb.

Then the squiggle went slowly up her spine.

She was in…lust? It spread into her breasts and licked inside the nipples.

She?

The ice maiden?

Surely not.

She smiled. She stretched her arms and lifted her legs and spread them widely. She watched Tom. He would be her first victim. Before this time, it had been she who'd been used. She would use…Tom.

Tom moved in his sleep. His breathing changed.

She considered him. Her eyes were lascivious. She licked her lips. Her eyes lifted to the man's face. His lips parted. He seemed intense. His breathing was as if he'd been backed into a portion of a cave by a standing bear.

She smiled. She was no bear.

Or…maybe she was actually a creature of prey. He was her prey.

She got up and went to the door and there was no lock on it. But there was a straight chair.

She tucked that under the knob quite skillfully. She went to the bed as she unbuttoned her blouse.

She hesitated soberly.

What was she doing? Had she gone berserk? The badly injured man was asleep! Helpless. He'd— Well, he had told her whenever she was interested to come to him, or call him or get in touch in whatever way she could. He was ready.

There *she* was, body hungry! How shocking! Not only *body hungry* but ready and eager—and the chair had barred the door!

She looked at Tom. The poor guy had just gone through a wringer by the murderer. He was out flat and dead asleep.

That was *his* problem.

She would just *use* him.

What if he couldn't...uh...rise to the occasion?

What if his damned sex was stubborn and selective? What if he was too hurt to be—even—interested? What if he was just lax and indifferent?

She went to the bed and looked at his face. He was frowning a tad. Nightmare?

He was dreaming *she* was *after* his body? Well, she *was!*

With some moxie from watching the male nurses, she held his arm and lifted it over so that he rolled over onto his back.

She looked at him. He was still sleeping. Out cold. Naked.

She smiled.

His sex was eager and excited and waving around quite shockingly for a man in that condition!

His lips parted. His breathing changed. It got a little rough.

She slid out of her panties, which were silk, and she put them on the chair. She took off her shoes. She slid in the diaphragm from her purse.

That was smart.

She gently climbed half over him and caught the wildly waving sex to guide it into her eager body.

She was thoughtfully wondering if it would be—and his good arm suddenly reached up, pulled her down on him and his lower body curled up to meet her!

She gasped.

He made a sound that was shockingly sexual delight, and he undulated slowly and with excessive pleasure.

He pulled her interesting, soft, chest down onto his chest with that one good arm and he said, "Move."

She thought he meant for her to get off his fragile body and said, "I'm sorry—"

He laughed in his throat in that wicked way only a man can do. He said, "Oh, baby—" He said, "Ahhhh."

He said, "Move only a little or I'll blow up like a volcano." He said, "I love you."

She said, "You tell all women that! You haven't even opened your eyes to *see* who is *on* you this way!"

He laughed. One never knows why in this world God ever allowed men to laugh that way. It's wicked and luring and shivers women's insides...low down in their pit.

He said, "Kiss me. Kiss me like you mean it."

She said, "Well, I was the one who started all this! Of *course* I 'mean' it!"

But his good arm brought her face down to his and he did the exceptional kissing. He was intrusive and fabulous! He did as he chose and he about drove her crazy!

They reached the heights and hung there in space

before they slid back down to earth and were again in his bed...her on top. She was quite disorganized. Her hair was all messed up. Her clothing was askew. And she was smiling.

He laughed softly.

She told him, "You just took over. I was going to be gentle and kind."

"You were."

"No. You did it all. I wasn't quite ready for such an—uh—encounter."

He was shocked. "You didn't enjoy it?"

She moved in a slight pushing wiggle on top of his body and she said, "It was awesome. I enjoyed it immensely."

"So'd I, you voracious, pushy woman."

"I wanted you."

"I've wanted you ever since I first saw you. What happened that you came on to me thisaway?"

"I don't know."

He sighed and hugged her, one armed. "Does this urge only come once in a lifetime?"

She considered and warned him, "It might not be that seldom."

"I think your just staying right there and holding what's left of me is very kind. But my sex is getting lax and shriveling up."

"How rude of it."

He sighed. "I have no control over it at all. It has a life of its own. You ought to see what excites him—and I'm not even interested!"

"How inter—or should I say 'a while ago?'"

"It was the one time it agreed with me." Tom sighed. "Life isn't easy for a man."

"Awwww."

Tom mentioned, "My sex is getting anxious and interested again. Could— I suppose, this soon, it'd be a drag?"

She said prissily, "Give me time to breathe."

Tom licked his lips and bit on his bottom lip as he inquired, "How much breathing do you do?"

Ellen lifted her eyebrows and looked down at Tom's face. She tilted her head as she inquired, "It's never been necessary. You must be overstudded?"

"I've never had this problem of my sex being so—pushy. I'm embarrassed."

She laughed. It was soft and smothered. She didn't move. She stayed on top of him on the bed.

Tom mentioned seriously, "We might be surprised. Who knows who all might come barging into this room?"

"I blocked the door."

He grinned and his chest rumbled a little as he laughed so slyly and so softly. His one good arm around her relentlessly, he asked, "Just what are you planning for this innocent child you've got trapped under you thisaway?"

"You're older than I, and I didn't have to do much of anything to get you. You're easy!" She tilted her head up so that she could look at him down her tiny nose.

He hugged her rather ruthlessly with that one good arm and he told her, "I'm gonna keep you, hear me?"

Airily, she retorted, "I've already uh—won—my take. I took you."

Tom said, "Mercy to goodness! If my mama ever finds this out, she'll faint right in the middle of everything. She's no discreet woman. She responds instantly. She'll faint and gasp and come to slowly as she asks my daddy, 'Did we really get *rid* of Tom?'"

Ellen nodded. "I'll say, 'Yep. It wasn't at all easy,' and I'll roll my eyes and sigh very dramatically."

"Wow."

She eased from him.

He objected.

She said, "I know how fragile you are. I shouldn't take such advantage of you."

"I don't mind a-tall! Cross my heart. Let's do it again."

"I have to adjust to being that invasive." She lifted a hand and said, "Oh, hush! I know. I *know*. But it *was* my idea! Just you remember that."

"I've waited for years."

"We've only known each other a little while."

"I fell in love with you when we went out on the deck and you sat at the table waiting for lunch or something."

"—to sit in the sunshine."

"Oh. I thought you were after—me."

"Not the first time."

Her mind must have gone on beyond and around because she *then* said, "What ever happened to that mouse in the cage in the kitchen?"

"We've looked. He was a barn mouse, and I suspect he skedaddled on back to where he belonged?"

She considered. "No sense of improvement? He was contented to be a stable mouse?"

"No élan at *all*."

She asked, "Élan? Now how'd you know such a word."

"My mama."

"I should have considered her influence. I've never really thought of you being led by another human."

"I'm not!"

She moved to release him and his one arm held her quickly. He said, "Stay with me."

"I'm squashing you. I need to let you breathe and move a little so that you can get better. If I stayed as an appendage, you might find it awkward."

"When I need to stand up?"

She corrected, "When people come into the room."

"That's very considerate of you. I suppose I should remember how ladylike you are."

"My mama taught me the rules." She began to release herself.

His arm brought her back to his body and he kissed her yet again. He allowed her some distance. Then he mentioned, "You're whisker burned. Nobody will be surprised. They'll think I gotcha."

"You did."

"I was a *victim!* I was helpless. You blocked the door and took *advantage* of me!"

She slid off the bed as she looked at the door then

at Tom. She lifted her eyebrows and retorted, "Of course. I did it. You're bed bound."

He sighed dramatically. "My whole, entire reputation is ruined! I've been...had."

She grinned very smugly. "Yes." She tilted her head and considered. "I'll see to it that somebody will have to knock on the door to find out how come it's locked to them. I'll open it. In five minutes *every single*—or married—person will *know* what went on in this room."

"I'm trapped." He sighed with some drama. "You'll *have* to marry me. My reputation is," he sighed again, "ruined."

"Yeah." She licked her lips and grinned. Then she combed her hair carefully. Put on lipstick with exquisite skill. She adjusted her clothing, shaking it out and smoothing it. She said, "I'm pure." With the most *wicked* glance at him he'd ever *seen!*

He threw out the hand of his good arm and said, "I'm gossip dust."

"Yep."

"You'll have to make me an honest man and—marry me."

With the last two words, he buckled back to being a man. His tone changed. His attention to her was riveted. He was deadly serious in the kindest, most charming manner. He watched her with intense attention. "Help me get out of bed so that I can get down on my good knee and propose properly."

She bit her bottom lip to control her smile, but her eyes sparkled with tender tears and danced as she said, "I suppose I should save your reputation."

"It would be kind of you. I wouldn't have to wear a hat over my face and sneak in and out of the house...if my mama and daddy even let me continue to stay there."

"They love you. If you were in trouble, they'd stand by you."

"Yeah."

Ellen became serious. "I love you, too."

"Enough? Or are you just tasting me."

"No. It's real. I love you."

"Come back in bed with me. Let me hold you against me."

She put up a hand as she said, "Don't tempt me. The crew will be in to wake you. I ought to rinse you off a little—"

"Okay."

"Do you know where I'm talking about?"

"I'd do anything to get you to rinse me off. Do it. The water will be cool and you'll have to kiss me to make me brave."

She considered. "I could do that."

"Okay. But you haven't much time. Hustle up, but take all the time you can."

"That's a little confusing. Hurry up and wait?"

"Hustle up...and be slow."

Ellen really smothered the laugh. Her eyes sparkled and she laughed silently.

"You're driving me crazy inside my skin."

"How weird. What's inside your...skin?"

"I'll show you."

"Whoops. Time is passing. I've got to tidy you. Be still and cooperate."

He muttered, "How can a man be still and still cooperate?"

"Hush."

Ellen washed his private parts first. She did his face next because there was a bit of her lipstick on his cheeks. Then she tidied the pillows and the sheet. He had already been naked from the exercise given him by the murderer.

When there was the knock on the door to waken Tom, Ellen had already released the door and was sitting calmly in the chair. She turned her head and said, "Shhhh. He's tired. The murderer just about killed him."

The intern laughed softly.

The whole entire *place* laughed because everyone had guessed what had happened. The intern was sure he was right, that the two had made love. He was positive. What else would have soothed the restless patient? The intern walked with some casual importance.

Tom smiled a whole lot. He was very different. He was distracted. He listened and licked his lips and smiled. Whoever was speaking with Tom knew his thinking was on someone else. But they knew who that someone was. It was Ellen.

Well, maybe not entirely, but Tom's attention was casual. He was more eager in getting his body back in shape. He endured the exercises more kindly.

The murderer who was the exerciser told Tom, "If you keep moving, they can't bury you...yet."

Rather drolly, Tom replied, "I appreciate that advice. Did you stay up all night fishing for that wisdom?"

The murderer's reply was: "Yeah."

But it was Ellen who mentioned once in a careful whisper when the staff thought Tom was supposed to be sleeping, "I'm glad that horse didn't step on that part of you."

Tom readily replied, "Me, too, and especially now. I love being inside you and feeling you squeeze me thataway."

She replied heartlessly aloof, "That's only exercise. It's good for my muscles."

His eyes overflowed with hilarity, and he tried not to snort and break the silence of the nap time.

He mentioned, "You be careful of making me laugh."

Airily, she replied, "I'm only being honest. What I say is basic."

And his own arm held her tightly as he lay under her and she moved. He gasped, "I like basic things."

She whispered, "Like—peanut butter?"

He opened his mouth on her cheek and rubbed his tongue on the fragile flesh. "Like that?" He whispered. Then he told her, "You taste like heaven, not peanut butter."

"Well, darn."

It was rather interesting how quickly Tom was improving. He slept better. He was relaxed. He was interested. He listened.

He and Ellen made love often and talked a lot. Of course, their conversations took place in whispers so as not to carry to other people's ears. They were very quiet. But their eyes sparkled and danced as they watched each other.

Tom said, "Let me hold your hand."

"I dare not get that close to you. You're a ravager!"

"Now, just you listen! I'm in bed with a useless arm and leg. Who's the ravager? Who was it that got on this bed and assaulted me?"

"Well, darn." She sighed in a rather eye-catching manner as she said, "I suppose *every*body knows I did it with you?"

"More than likely."

Slowly her face sobered. She finally looked at Tom. She said, "I was careless with myself."

"Not you. Phillip."

"I allowed it."

"What choice did you have?"

She considered that time with Phillip. "Not very much." She turned her head and looked out of the low window across the bed. "I was somewhat shocked."

"Like I was—not long ago when you assaulted me?"

Ellen gasped in genuine shock. "I hadn't thought... I didn't know..."

Tom laughed. "You were heaven!"

"But— I hadn't realized—"

"Hush, woman, I wasn't serious. I was just teasing."

"How could you be that harsh with me when you know what a life I've led?"

He was serious and concerned. "What do you mean—what sort of life *have* you—led?"

She turned to the window and her back was to Tom. She folded her arms in front of her body, blocking from him the outline of her breasts. She said sadly, "It doesn't matter."

She ignored the intake of his breath as she turned and walked to the door of his room. She looked at him seriously and ignored his urgent voice as he said, "Listen, honey, you're off on a roller coaster that has nothing to do with anything current."

She looked at him very seriously. Then she said, "Yes."

He urged, "What's that mean?"

Her gaze was steady and serious. "I understand." She moved to the door and put her hand on the doorknob.

He tried to curl up to sit up. He urged, "Don't leave me."

"One of the other women will be glad to come by."

"I don't want any other woman. I want you."

"One female is just like another."

He was extremely serious. "Are you saying I'm like Phillip?"

She tilted her head. "You're slower, and I had the time to enjoy you."

"Don't leave me."

"I'm going back to the house. I'll be in touch."

She turned and went out of the hospital room's door as Tom said, "Wait!"

She paused and just looked at him. Then she said, "Get the female nurse." And she left.

Ten

It is a serious thing to a man to be stoved up and abed when a woman walks out on him. What is he to do?

No smart man asks another *man* to go after his love and bring her back. But then, what woman would do that?

What woman would go out after another woman who had just discarded a man?

He phoned Lu over at Rip's place. He told her, "You've got to help me. I need you right this minute. I have no idea who all is listening in, come over to the hospital and I'll tell you what all you need to know."

Lu groaned something about the male population in its entirety and hung up.

That shocked Tom and he hung up! But then he immediately called Lu back.

That quick, the line was riveted with chatter! Just like that! Didn't anybody have enough to do that they had to hang on the line? Good gravy! A man is endlessly coping with idle, visiting people.

He tried to call Ellen, but was unable to get through on the phone. Tom decided to go up to the main house and see her for himself. It was important. He needed to stop her successive atomic blowups as soon as possible.

A man who is bed bound with a broken leg and arm is not one that *any*body wants to go on off on his own.

The head medic said to Tom, "You aren't yet mended enough to go leaping off along the way back home. You have to stay here a while longer."

Tom told the top medic, "Go to hell."

The man replied kindly, "See if you can get up— by yourself."

That was not at all kind, but the staff did get testy after a while.

Tom heaved up and he did try.

The medical head said, "See to it that you don't louse up that leg. Be careful. No! Don't *do* that! Only an imbecile would try something like that. Cut it out!"

Sweating, determined, teeth clenched, struggling, Tom did try.

The muscle builder murderer was at the door and when he could stand no further push on his fragile patient, he brushed past the top medic and said, "Here. This is how it's done." And he helped Tom.

The senior medic watched without intruding or saying anything. He just watched.

As Tom struggled to move *from* the room, he told the murderer, "I can't walk clear over home."

The murderer replied, "I gotta car."

White faced, grim, the patient said, "Thank God."

The murderer took that slot and replied, "No problem."

Tom said through sweat and clenched teeth—he hurt—"You're not God."

The murderer just said a nothing, "Oh." He was being tolerant.

They struggled out of the small, animal shared "hospital." The murderer propped Tom against a door and went to bring his car to that door. It would save some distance for Tom.

With the murderer gone and his fragile body leaned against the doorjamb, Tom closed his eyes and just did not move one bit. He was white faced. His blood was all in his feet. He was in a cold sweat.

A nurse came along and stopped with great drama. She gasped, "*How* in this *world* did you get out *here?*"

Tom told her, "Be quiet."

She was appalled. She said, "This is *not* the thing to *do,* you foolish, foolish man!"

"Hush."

The murderer interrupted the nurse's gasp of indignation as he drove his car right up to the door. There were no steps for Tom to maneuver.

Tom didn't move. The murderer came and helped Tom to the car.

The nurse went away yelling, "One of the humans is escaping!"

Tom got into the car with the murderer's help. Tom was carefully eased into the back seat of the car. Then the murderer drove up to the big house.

Tom said nothing the entire way.

The murderer asked, "Who're you looking for?"

"Ellen."

"That little thing? She ain't—"

"Hush!"

The murderer figured it out. "You like her."

"Yeah."

"Oh." And the murderer was silent. Who can figure out people? So the murderer's interest was triggered and he maneuvered the car very carefully to a side door. He knew the layout of the house…that was the easiest way.

Apparently everyone in the big house knew of Tom's escape from the hospital and his duly arrival at the house.

Ellen was the most appalled. She came out to the car and leaned over to see if Tom had actually done something that stupid. He had. She said, "What on *earth* made you do this stupid thing?"

"I was afraid I'd lost you."

"Good heavens! One woman isn't worth all this effort!"

"You are."

"No. I've decided I'm healed and it's time for me

to move on.'' She was aloof and quite cool about the words.

The murderer was between the couple by then, and he was turning his head from one to the other as if he was at a tennis match. He was silent.

Tom told Ellen, ''I was so anxious to get to you that I forgot my body isn't well enough to be doing this. I'm about—''

He fainted.

The murderer thought Tom was especially smart to handle the woman in that manner. But then he looked at the milk white face of the man and thought maybe he really *had* fainted! He took over.

That's when the murderer knew Ellen really loved Tom. She became appalled, hysterical and frantic. She thought Tom was dead—and it was her fault!

The murderer said offhand in his regular voice, ''He's okay.''

Ellen was just about hysterical. She pulled Tom's head against her breast and wailed.

Beyond them, John Keeper had grabbed his wife, Mina, back to him and kept her in his arms. The tears rolled down her face but she was silent and still.

That was when the murderer looked around at all the frozen people who were witness to this drama. But it was only then that the murderer understood that it *was* a drama! He watched. Nobody moved.

Ellen quite obviously thought Tom was dead. She held him against her and wept.

The murderer again said to Ellen, ''He's okay. He's just not used to getting around this much yet.''

She looked at the murderer and begged, "Help me get him to bed."

The murderer said, "Okay." Then without any seeming effort, he lifted the bulk of Tom into his arms. One arm was out stiff in its cast and one leg was straight in that cast. With that done, the murderer stood there. He asked, "Where'd you want him?"

Ellen replied, "My room."

Nobody said nothing a-tall, but the murderer did inquire, "Where's that?"

Ellen replied instantly, "This way."

She led the way and all the people followed along after the murderer who carried the unconscious Tom quite easily.

The murderer was the one who put Tom into Ellen's room—and on her bed. He tidied the patient. He left the better blood colored man to the hovering woman. He said to her, "If you need me, just whistle."

Her big, serious eyes came to the murderer and she asked, "What sort of whistle?"

He put the tip of his thumb and middle finger into his mouth and blew a very subtle whistle. "That's if I'm in the hall. If I'm farther, you really blow, and I'll come arunning."

"Thank you."

The murderer smiled. Then he went into the hall and observed the people there. He told the Keepers, "Tom's okay."

John smiled but Mina couldn't stop the tears. Her husband held her. The others spoke softly and reassuringly to each other. Some left, some went into the living room to sit and discuss what all had happened. And there were those who actually went back to work.

Tom was better than he pretended. He loved being in her room. In her bed. She would crawl in after her bath, and she'd be stark naked. He'd gasp. She'd laugh down in her throat.

Tom said, "I believe it will be some long time until I'll say I'm well enough to get out of bed."

"Oh?" she inquired. "Just what did you have in mind to do—in bed?"

He had to show her what all. He was very particular, careful, slow and scandalous!

Her body loved it all. Her laugh was soft and personal and wonderful to his ears.

He slept a lot.

How strange to see a sleeping man who couldn't quit smiling. Odd.

One brief time when Ellen was out of the room, Tom told the murderer, "I have to salute you. You are the most clever man I've ever encountered. Thank you."

The murderer smiled.

Tom then looked at the murderer and inquired, "What *is* your name?"

"Ralph."

Tom said, "Ahhh," and nodded. Then he asked, "May I call you by name?"

The murderer whose name was Ralph smiled but

he licked his lips as if he wasn't amused. He said, "Sure."

Being in Ellen's room was heaven. She slept carefully next to him as he recovered...one way or another. She was so kind. But Tom still had Ralph bathe him.

Ellen said, "If I can do all those other things with you, how come I can't give you a bath?"

He explained gently, "We'd never get out of the room!"

She grinned and lowered her eyelids.

He said, "How come you wanted to leave me?"

"I thought you were just...using me."

"Now you know how much I care about you? How much I love you?"

"Yes."

"Will you marry me?"

"I think maybe I'll just do that."

"I love you, Ellen."

"Oh, Tom, how could I be so lucky as to have found you?"

"I think it was a miracle."

A few days later, the still fragile Tom and the gentle Ellen were on the side porch in the shade. They were reading and sharing what they found interesting. The time was precious, lazy and very nice. Tom was on a lounger and there was an umbrella over him to keep the sun under control.

The murderer, Ralph, came out and with some distaste said to Ellen, "There's a guy who's come to see you. I don't like him. Why don't I just tell him you're not here."

She asked with some curiosity, "Who is it?"

"He says his name is Phillip. He didn't give me a last n—"

"Phillip? *Phillip!* He's *here?*"

Tom looked over at Ellen. He understood this was an important moment for her. And there he was, still in casts. How was he to defend his right to this woman if that other man could upset her that much?

Tom tried to get up off the lounge. He said, "I want to shatter his face."

She smiled at her love. "I wouldn't have you touch him."

Those very words she said to Tom scared the—

But she continued, "You're mountains taller than he. I won't have you dirty your hands on such."

Ralph said, "Let me. I know exactly how to do something like that. We learn to handle recalcitrant pilgrims."

Tom gasped, "You're dangerous with *others?*"

Ralph smiled in a wonderfully nasty way as he said, "Yeah."

Twice shaking one finger at him, Ellen told Ralph, "You don't touch anyone unless I tell you. Understand?"

Ralph smiled not at her but over at the fragile *Tom*—sharing the anticipation of a revenge and said, "Yes'um."

"I mean it!" she warned.

Ralph nodded with total innocence as he promised, "I hear you." That was no promise at all.

It was—the murderer—Ralph who went out to escort the visitor Phillip out to the lounger and the beauty who was with him.

Tom felt excessively possessive.

The guest came walking toward them. Phillip was tall and his features were perfect. His body was perfect. He walked like a man. He acted like a perfect one.

Tom tasted stomach bile. What an awful time for a man to be hampered by casts. How was he to defend his woman and give her the satisfaction of rearranging Phillip's face?

Tom looked over at the calm murderer. Ralph wasn't involved enough to really wipe the dust with this approaching damned snot.

Tom sat. He had no choice.

Ellen also sat. She observed this person who approached. What had she seen in him? Why had she ever cared…about him? How interesting.

But the murderer stood blocking his chair. It was not in a courteous manner. He was dangerous. He was like an uncoiling, very chancy spring.

That did catch Phillip's eye. But he discarded the stranger's conduct and looked past the invalid to Ellen. "Hello!" he smiled and was confident of a courteous greeting in return.

She said nothing. She sat and watched Phillip. It was as if she monitored him. Debit side.

How strange, she thought, to meet an old lover and wonder what the dickens she'd ever seen in such a wimpy mess?

Phillip found a chair and brought it over to the

three. Two sitting and one standing. The standing one was not being courteous. He looked hostile.

Phillip smiled somewhat at the hostile one, then dismissed him entirely and looked at Ellen. That meant he'd not only discarded Ralph, he ignored the invalid entirely as no problem.

Phillip said, "You're looking well." He smiled.

Ellen didn't move a muscle. She considered Phillip. She wondered what about him had lured her? She blinked her eyes thoughtfully and considered him further.

There was silence.

Phillip looked around and smiled. He said, "How'd you find such a place? It's perfect for a holiday."

No one replied.

But the three all had their eyes riveted on Phillip. That was obvious.

Phillip was confident. He asked, "You gonna invite me to lunch?"

Ellen gasped.

The two watching men said in unison as if practiced, "No."

Phillip laughed! And he had the stupid audacity to exclaim, "I'm no threat."

While the two men growled, Ellen said, "No."

Now, did she say "no" that the intruder was no threat? Or was she saying "no" to the two hostile men?

Neither of the hostile ones cared which she meant, they just watched the invader...unkindly.

Ellen took a deep, slow, patient breath. Women

simply do not need to deal with men who are hostile to one another. If Phillip had been hostile to *her,* she might have been glad the two protectors were there. But Phillip was never hostile. He had left her. Vanished.

She inquired kindly, "What brought you out this way? How do you know the Keepers?"

"Your mother wouldn't tell me where you were, so I asked your friend, Jeannie. She told me." He smiled confidently.

Ellen considered their surprise guest. She asked, "Why are you here?"

"I just thought I'd check up on our kid."

It was probably the "our" kid that sent Ellen— emotionally—right up to the top of the oak beside them. Her breath changed. Her eyes changed. She became a very basic woman.

But it was Tom who said in a deadly voice, "Why are you curious…now?"

Phillip smiled kindly and explained. "I've had a vasectomy." He smiled just a tad as if they would protest such an action. No one commented, so Phillip exclaimed, "I remembered you and wondered what you did with our kid."

He'd again said…*our* kid.

That was probably the bit that sent Ellen right over the edge. She breathed quite obviously. She was trembling. She was furious!

So was Tom.

He made a foolish effort and rose to his feet! He stood there—riveted!

Ralph said to Tom, "Allow me." Then he moved toward Phillip.

Ellen said calmly, "No, Ralph. Sit down, Tom."

They both looked at the woman. She was calm. She looked at them quite in control not only of herself, but of *them!*

That irritated the hell out of them.

She watched Ralph help Tom to sit down. Tom was not in that mood and was difficult. Ralph insisted. Tom had no choice. He was furious!

Then Ralph sat beside Tom. He looked at Ellen.

But Ellen had risen and walked over to Phillip. She said, "The baby died inside me."

She quit. She didn't leak a tear. She was calm.

It was interesting to see that Phillip was upset. He said, "Damn!" He said, "I hadn't known." He said, "I'm very sorry about this. I'll never have any kids I guess." He sighed and frowned at nothing. Then he pushed up from the chair and said, "I'll go along. Goodbye."

And he left!

Not one of Phillip's words was about the baby *or* Ellen. That selfish man thought only of himself. Ellen watched him leave. How remarkable that she had ever been involved with such a selfish man.

Ellen tilted her head. She smiled. She looked at her love and said, "I'm free!" She lifted her arms and tilted back her head.

"You—loved—him?"

Ellen looked at Tom. She didn't even know that Ralph had followed their visitor to be sure he left.

Ellen told Tom. "No. I love you. I—hush—I

hadn't known what love really was. Sex. But what I feel from you and in myself is more than just sex. You love me.''

''I've mentioned that on occasion.'' He was careful and deadly serious. Women are another race altogether. Men never really understand them. Even *men* know that.

She looked at Tom and her eyes filled with tears as she smiled at him.

He groaned and said, ''Ellen—''

''I love you.'' She said that. She sat there, looking at him. And she didn't move at all.

He shook his head, suffering, and he asked, ''How can I get to you? Can you come closer so I can hold you?''

She smiled. ''I could sit by you and walk with you and talk with you and never touch you or lie in bed with you—and I would still love you.''

In a rough, emotional voice, he said, ''That's what I feel about you. I love you, Ellen.''

''It's what love means.'' She sat and smiled at Tom. ''I might not have realized what we have—if Phillip hadn't come and made you clear to me.''

Puzzled, Tom frowned as he asked, ''Made *me* clear to you?''

''You're not only a lover, you're a man. You're by me. It isn't just sex. You love *me.*''

He watched her, frowning, and said, ''You didn't understand before this?''

''I thought I was just a good toy for you.''

Tom sighed with *great* endurance and looked off at the sky quite disgruntled.

She laughed in her throat.

People can do that. Laugh that way. Soft and deep in their throats. Both men and women. It raises the hair roots on the other person and shivers their insides quite noticeably. It causes a whole lot of intimate encounters.

But what the two had encountered wasn't just sex. It was love. The mating of two lovers. It is the ultimate. The sharing of such emotion. Such pleasure. It is superb.

It also causes children because the entwined adults just don't consider the risk.

However, it is not the selfishness of Phillip who didn't even notice he had a partner. He'd used her. That's a whole, entire other thing. It isn't love. It's using.

With Tom, Ellen found out about love. About caring. About sharing. About laughter. About concern. It took them a while to understand there were other people on this planet.

Everybody knew about Tom and Ellen. They watched and smiled. They exchanged looks with their mates and laughed…remembering.

Ellen was progressing. She was eating better. Tom was thinner. In their room, Tom told her, "You're a whole lot softer than you used to be."

She was surprised. "I work like a Trojan! How in this world could I be softer?"

He said, "Maybe my body was feeling wrong. Let me touch you and see?"

His hands went around on her and their breathing changed. Deep in a serious kiss, their eyes would come unfocused and they never saw the tolerant people who went around them and left them alone.

He said to her, "Your chest is getting pushy." And his hands indicated the area being discussed.

Ellen looked down between their clamped bodies, seeing nothing but squashed together bodies. She said, "Well, darn."

In a harshly breathing manner, he said kindly, "I'll adjust them."

She inquired perfectly logically, "How?"

His reply was never solid conversation or instructions. He'd say, "I'll…think of…something. I'll…work on them. Exercise."

But they didn't do much else. However, exercise *is* exercise. He didn't sleep much, since he mostly thought about her. And thinking about her did not put him to sleep. He begged the doctors that he could again jog. They gave him rubber pullers to use as muscle builders. It didn't help very much. He was skinny.

She slept the sleep of repletion.

One day as they met in the hall, she smiled at Tom, as she stood in front of him and his crutches with her hands behind her back.

He growled inside his throat. "What are you up to…now."

Not even a question.

She said, "I want to marry you."

His eyes slowly became naked. How many times had he asked her that very thing? He had to breathe through his mouth because his nose wouldn't take that much air and his lungs needed the air or he'd faint.

She understood that he was boggled. She smiled and tears filled her eyes. "I love you."

"My God, Ellen. I'm not sure I can handle all this standing up thisaway. I think I ought to sit down."

"I'll go find you a chair—"

"Let's go to the floor library—"

She laughed so softly. "Okay."

That's where they found Ciggie, researching some word.

"Hi, you kids. Whatcha looking for?"

Ellen said, "He's going to propose." She said that as if it was the most natural thing *ever!*

Ciggie whooped—

Ellen put a finger up to her mouth. "Don't tell... yet."

Ciggie swatted Tom's shoulder and she went on out of the library.

Tom closed the door after her. He turned his naked eyes over to his love as he took a key out and locked the door.

She said, "Oh-oh."

He finally smiled. He sighed. He said, "I gotcha."

"Yep."

"Oh, Ellen—"

"You haven't proposed as yet. Not officially."

"How do I do that?"

"You have to get down on your knees—"

They both looked at his not quite healed leg.

She said, "Well, we'll postpone that for a while. It can just be verbal."

"I love you. I want to marry you."

She sighed with rolled eyes and instructed him, "You're *supposed* to say that I'm the most gorgeous woman you've *ever* seen and you'll die without me."

"How'd you know that?"

"Don't you read *any*thing?"

"Tell me what all to say to—"

She did that. And he said all those things right after she did. Then he went off on his own. He told her how beautiful she was. How he'd watched her when she was so ill. How he cared about her.

Tears came but her smile just went on and on. Her hands on him were so gentle. She loved the feel of his body on hers. That was when she understood that she was flat out on the sofa, mostly naked and being—loved.

The whole entire Keeper Place went berserk. It was like they'd all been surprised! How could they be? Who all didn't know?

The celebration of the engagement was a buster. The huge Keeper house was jammed! Now, how could *that* many people get there that quick? They just did.

It was almost a riot. All the men insisted on a kiss. Ellen gave tiny little cheek kisses. She explained, "He'll kill any man who tries for my mouth."

Well, the guys could all understand that selfishness.

By the time the wedding gown was made-to-order and delivered, Tom was out of the splints. Of course, he walked carefully. His arm worked quite well. He could use it to hug his bride.

His leg was—well—it was coming along. It didn't deter him in any way with Ellen.

The whole, entire area was vulnerable to emotion and love. It was a happy time…for them all.

*   *   *   *   *

Watch for Lass Small's next book in March '99 from Silhouette Desire.

INTIMATE MOMENTS®
Silhouette®

Coming in October from
Silhouette Intimate Moments...

BRIDES OF THE NIGHT

Silhouette Intimate Moments fulfills your wildest
wishes in this compelling new in-line collection
featuring two very memorable men...tantalizing,
irresistible men who exist only in the darkness
but who hunger for the light of true love.

TWILIGHT VOWS
by Maggie Shayne

The unforgettable WINGS IN THE NIGHT miniseries
continues with a vampire hero to die for and the
lovely mortal woman who will go to any lengths to
save their unexpected love.

MARRIED BY DAWN
by Marilyn Tracy

Twelve hours was all the time this rogue vampire
had to protect an innocent woman. But was
marriage his only choice to keep her safe—if not
from the night...then from himself?

Look for BRIDES OF THE NIGHT this October,
wherever Silhouette books are sold.

Silhouette®

Look us up on-line at: http://www.romance.net   SIMBON

Take 2 bestselling love stories FREE

Plus get a FREE surprise gift!

Special Limited-Time Offer

Mail to Sihouette Reader Service™

> P.O. Box 609
> Fort Erie, Ontario
> L2A 5X3

YES! Please send me 2 free Silhouette Desire® novels and my free surprise gift. Then send me 6 brand-new novels every month, which I will receive months before they appear in bookstores. Bill me at the low price of $3.49 each plus 25¢ delivery and GST*. That's the complete price, and a saving of over 10% off the cover prices—quite a bargain! I understand that accepting the books and gift places me under no obligation ever to buy any books. I can always return a shipment and cancel at any time. Even if I never buy another book from Silhouette, the 2 free books and the surprise gift are mine to keep forever.

326 SEN CH7V

Name	(PLEASE PRINT)	
Address		Apt. No.
City	Province	Postal Code

This offer is limited to one order per household and not valid to present Silhouette Desire® subscribers. *Terms and prices are subject to change without notice. Canadian residents will be charged applicable provincial taxes and GST.

CDES-98 ©1990 Harlequin Enterprises Limited

Bestselling author
Joan Elliott Pickart launches
Silhouette's newest cross-line promotion

with
THE
RANCHER
AND
THE
AMNESIAC
BRIDE
Special Edition,
October 1998

Josie Wentworth of the oil-rich Oklahoma Wentworths
knew penthouse apartments and linen finery—not
working ranches...and certainly *not* remote,
recalcitrant ranchers! But one conk to the head and
one slight case of amnesia had this socialite beauty
sharing time and tangling sheets with the cowboy
least likely to pop the question....

And don't miss **The Daddy and the Baby Doctor**
by Kristin Morgan, when FOLLOW THAT BABY!
continues in Silhouette Romance in November 1998!

Available at your favorite retail outlet.

Look us up on-line at: http://www.romance.net   SSEFTB1

MATERNITY LEAVE

Coming September 1998

Three delightful stories about the blessings
and surprises of "Labor" Day.

TABLOID BABY by Candace Camp

She was whisked to the hospital in the nick of time....

THE NINE-MONTH KNIGHT
by Cait London

A down-on-her-luck secretary is experiencing
odd little midnight cravings....

THE PATERNITY TEST by Sherryl Woods

The stick turned blue before her
biological clock struck twelve....

*These three special women are very pregnant...and very
single, although they won't be either for too much longer,
because baby—and Daddy—are on their way!*

Available at your favorite retail outlet.

Look us up on-line at: http://www.romance.net   PSMATLEV

SILHOUETTE®

Desire®

presents a compelling
new series from
Maureen Child...

THE
BACHELOR
BATTALION

*These irresistibly sexy marines live hard—
and love even harder.*

THE LITTLEST MARINE (SD #1167, September '98)
Harding Casey was divine in uniform—and out of it! Which
explained why this handsome hunk was to become a father—
and just before he was set to sail overseas. Would mother and
child pull rank and have this soldier taking leave...for good?

THE NON-COMMISSIONED BABY
(SD #1174, October '98)
When **Jeff Ryan** faced his toughest assignment yet—daddy
to a six-month-old—he enlisted the expert help of Laura
Morgan...a woman whose lovely form could stop a battle-
ship. But could it anchor the heart of one tough marine?

And find out which marine will
explore uncharted territory in...
THE OLDEST LIVING MARRIED VIRGIN
(SD #1180, November '98)

Available at your favorite retail outlet.

Silhouette®

Look us up on-line at: http://www.romance.net

SDBBAT

#1 *New York Times* bestselling author

NORA ROBERTS

**Presents a brand-new book in the
beloved MacGregor series:**

THE WINNING HAND
(SSE#1202)

October 1998 in

$\mathcal{Silhouette}$®SPECIAL EDITION®

Innocent Darcy Wallace needs Mac Blade's protection in
the high-stakes world she's entered. But who will protect
Mac from the irresistible allure of this vulnerable beauty?

**Coming in March, the much-anticipated novel,
THE MacGREGOR GROOMS
Also, watch for the MacGregor stories
where it all began!**

**December 1998:
THE MacGREGORS: Serena—Caine**

**February 1999:
THE MacGREGORS: Alan—Grant**

**April 1999:
THE MacGREGORS: Daniel—Ian**

Available at your favorite retail outlet, only from

▼ $\mathcal{Silhouette}$®
™

Look us up on-line at: http://www.romance.net   SSEMACS1

COMING NEXT MONTH